AF278914

Pulled Over

Chapter 1

OH, CRAP! Sunny glanced in her review mirror to see a cop car pull up behind her old Chevy truck. Her gaze darted back to the red light above her. It had to be the longest light on Main Street, and she began to get nervous. She chanced another glance in her mirror, thankful for the oversized shades shielding her eyes. At least he wouldn't notice she kept looking at him.

Dudley only had three cops in their piss-ant, small country town, and word was out that a new one had just been hired. It had to be the cop behind her because she didn't recognize him as Joe, Stan or Mark, two of which she'd gone to high school with. Joe, the oldest, had been a cop for as long as Sunny could remember.

Was the damn light stuck? She began to feel sweat gather between her breasts, and took a few deliberate breaths to calm her racing heart. If he didn't notice her expired tag it would be a miracle, and Sunny suspected it was standard procedure when a cop pulled up behind someone at a light that they automatically checked the tag. Maybe the new guy would forget to check.

She glanced at the cop again. From what Sunny could see, the man was big and hunky in a Tatum Channing way and even had the same color hair and style. She wondered what color his eyes were, behind the aviator style sunglasses he was wearing. His square boned jaw looked hard, until his lips turned up in a slow smile telling Sunny that he knew she was watching him. She quickly looked down as if he could see her eyes. *Crap!*

The light finally changed and Sunny accelerated. She didn't dare glance behind her again, but she was aware the cop was right on her ass. Had he noticed her tag? Lord, she hoped not. She couldn't afford a ticket. At least there wasn't another light to worry about, as she headed in the direction that would take her out of town. She was careful to watch her speed, praying when they came up to the small police station that he'd pull into the designated parking spot. Only he didn't.

Damn it! Why is he still behind me? Sunny was forced to stop when she came up to a cross walk, and she saw Mrs. Hammond step off the curb. Of all people! It had to be sixty-six year old, three-hundred pound Margaret Hammond who moved with all the speed of a snail. Sunny shut her eyes with frustration, and began to count. She might as well just go up to the cop behind her and tell him about the tag.

"Hello, dear!"

Sunny opened her eyes, and smiled. "Hi Mrs. Hammond, I see you're out getting your daily exercise. How are you doing?"

"Fine, dear, just fine." She kept on shuffling, barely picking up her feet.

As soon as Mrs. Hammond was clear of Sunny's truck, Sunny put her foot down on the gas, jerked forward, and came to a halt. *Oh. My. God.* Can it get any worse? A glance in her review mirror revealed the handsome cop behind her was laughing. Sunny clenched her teeth and turned the key, swearing beneath her breath at her traitor truck.

The engine roared to life but by now there were two other people in the crosswalk and she could do nothing but wait. She grabbed the material of her blouse and fluffed, feeling some relief, wishing her air conditioner worked. It wasn't as if she couldn't afford a new vehicle, but old blue had been handed down from one sibling to another in her family, until it was finally hers. It had sentimental value.

At last she was moving again. Main Street ended, and Sunny was traveling the two-lane country road home. It was quiet, and not as busy as it used to be before the new highway went in a couple years ago. The countryside was dotted with old, northern homes, and fenced in pastures. Most empty now, but when she'd been growing up the fields had been filled with dairy cows, and corn. The old ways had been replaced with progress, and most of the country-folk worked in the surrounding towns.

Sunny had tried city-life but she'd hated it. She was a country girl at heart, and she liked her small town where everyone knew everyone. Glancing up, she was dismayed to find the cop was still on her tail. Was it too much to hope that they just happened to be going the same way? Surely he would have stopped her by now if he'd noticed her tag.

As if sensing her worry, he turned on his siren, and Sunny reluctantly pulled off the road onto the shoulder. Since they'd reached the old abandoned Miller house she continued down the dirt drive so that if anyone happened to pass by she wouldn't be seen. Small towns had people with big mouths, and she didn't want to become the topic of gossip until something new came along.

She drew to a halt, cut off the ignition, and waited.

Chapter 2

The cop pulled his cruiser behind Sunny, and surprised her by switching off the siren and the engine. She watched him in her mirror, noticing that he was talking on his radio. He was probably calling in her tag. She pressed her lips, wishing she hadn't let her tag expire, but it was too late to do anything about it now. Movement drew her attention once more to her review mirror. She watched as the door opened and he stepped out.

Ohmygod! The man was hot! He was easily six feet four of solid muscle poured into a navy blue police uniform. The sight of all that defined muscle and the tightness of the material over his zipper area drew a response from Sunny's body she wasn't prepared for. He looked like he was strong enough to take on an army or at the very least a girl with curves, which she had plenty of. She caught her breath as he slowly walked up to her truck.

Before he reached her door, she opened a couple more buttons on her blouse and parted the material so he would have a better view of her large breasts. She was proud of their fullness, even if she was a little ashamed that she was using them as a means to possibly talk him out of giving her a ticket. Sunny imagined a cop as impressive as him had tits and ass thrown in his face all the time.

She glanced in her side view mirror, and ran her tongue over her full lips. Then she fluffed her long blonde hair. By the time the cop reached her door her nipples were tingling and as hard as pebbles, but it was worse than that. She had to squeeze her thighs together to appease the mild buzzing in her clit.

"Ma'am," he said as he stopped by her opened window. His voice was deep, and a little gravely, running over Sunny like warm, thick honey.

"Hi, officer." She glanced at his nametag. "Officer Steele." Sunny offered him a warm smile. "Was I doing something wrong?"

He waited a few seconds. "Could you please remove your sunglasses, ma'am."

Her mouth dropped with surprise. "Why would I want to do that? Are they against the law?"

"No, ma'am. But I'd like to see your eyes when I'm talking to you."

Oh. Sunny had to wonder what he would do if she refused. "What if I said no, officer?" She knew she was playing with fire. She couldn't see his eyes either, but his mouth was tight and his jaw was set. Her response obviously annoyed him. Deciding she'd never get out of a ticket by aggravating him, she gave in and removed her glasses slowly.

His slow grin might be sexy as hell, but only pissed Sunny off because he was using his authority to control her. Still, she kept her composure. She looked up at him and batted her baby blues enticingly. "Better?" she asked coyly.

Officer Steele ignored her attempt at flirtation. "Do you know why I pulled you over?" he asked in a no nonsense tone.

"My expired tag?" Sunny chewed on her bottom lip, wishing she could see where his eyes were focused. She took a deep breath, knowing it would push her breasts up and out. She'd bet a hundred dollars his gaze was glued to her cleavage.

"That and you have a taillight out."

"What?" Sunny didn't know about the taillight. "Which one?"

"Passenger side," he said, "Can I please see your driver's license?"

Sunny reached for her small purse on the seat next to her. She dug around the contents, pulling out several things that got in the way, until she finally located her license in a side pocket. "I've changed a little since this was taken."

Sunny had always been a curvaceous woman, which her almost six-foot frame carried well, but the license she'd handed the cop was about six years old. She'd had shorter, darker hair back then.

Officer Steele remained quiet, turned and walked back to his cruiser. Sunny released a heavy sigh, watching his sexy gait take him back to his car. Her gaze lingered on his ass. *Lord, he has a nice body!* She made the mistake of envisioning what she'd like to do to him but it only made her hotter. Before she knew it her hand was gliding down her body to the spot between her legs. It hadn't been that long since she'd had sex, just that morning, but she was tingling and wanted a cock inside her so badly that she was suddenly wondering how she could get Officer Steele to comply.

Her purse was still on her lap. She spied a small roll on perfume bottle and quickly applied some to her cleavage, and her wrists. Something told her this cop went by the book and she would have to apply herself a little harder to get what she wanted. She made sure to fluff her blouse right before he reached her window, knowing he'd get a whiff of her perfume.

"Here's your license, ma'am."

Sunny took it from him and then watched as he reached for the pen and pad in his upper pocket. She swallowed hard, realizing what he was about to do. Desperation forced her to do something slutty. "God, it's so darn hot today!" She pulled her blouse away from her sticky skin. With his height advantage, she knew he'd get a good view of two forty double D's barely stuffed into a lacy bra.

His mouth twitched, as if he was trying to contain another grin. He flipped the pad opened, and clicked his pen as he got ready to write.

"Officer!" Sunny said in a rushed tone to get his attention. She knew once he started writing it would be all over. "Please don't give me a ticket."

He hesitated. "And why not?" He cocked his head to the side, and waited.

"Well, I, um," Once again Sunny wished he'd remove his glasses. "I promise to take care of the tag and light by this weekend."

He shook his head slowly. "Not good enough." He prepared to write a second time.

"Wait, I, surely there's something I can do in exchange for you, ah, just giving me a verbal warning this time." Sunny couldn't see his eyes but he sure as hell could see hers. To make sure there were no doubts to what she meant she slowly ran her gaze down the front of him. She couldn't believe she was acting so brazenly.

"Are you bribing me, ma'am?" Officer Steele removed his sunglasses, and fixed his stony black eyes on hers.

Sunny was mesmerized by the look on his chiseled face. It was all hard, and there was a muscle twitching in his jaw, yet there was something about him that said he wasn't immune to her charms either. She feigned innocence. "I would never bribe an officer of the law." Once more she let her gaze move down his body, this time stopping on the front of his pants.

A river of molten heat enveloped her when she realized he had an erection. Going by the size of the bulge behind his zipper he was thick and long. Liquid warmth slid into Sunny's panties as she imagined Officer Steele ramming his cock into her cunt. What would it take to make him lose control?

Without warning she saw his gaze narrow on something on the seat next to her. "Is that pot?"

Sunny glanced at what he was looking at. She couldn't help it, she laughed. "No, I don't do drugs. That's catnip." She made a move to pick up the small plastic bag.

"Don't move!"

Officer Steele's harsh command caused her to freeze. "Step out of the car, please."

"But–"

"I said step out of the car!"

He backed up as Sunny opened her door and got out. She was small compared to him, and had to glance up a long way to meet his sharp gaze. A breeze picked up her long hair, bringing it forward to rest against her breast. At the same time her blouse separated even more where she'd unbuttoned it. Officer Steele's gaze moved over her, from her exposed cleavage, down to her cut off shorts, naked thighs, legs and back up again. Then without warning he grabbed Sunny, swung her around and slammed her up against the front of her truck.

She gasped loudly. "What are you doing?"

His tone was close to the back of her neck. Sunny could feel his warm breath stir the fine hairs there. "I'm going to frisk you." He moved, and suddenly his mouth was against her ear. "And then I'm going to fuck you."

Chapter 3

Please, yes! Sunny couldn't help thinking. He was so damn sexy, and she was getting more turned on by the moment. She didn't move, though. The way he'd pushed her against the truck, his demeanor warned her that he liked control and had to do things his way. That was just fine with her. She liked a man who dominated. Sex with him was going to be mind-blowing, and Sunny was already trembling.

Suddenly his hands were on her shoulders. Sunny wanted to lean back into him, maybe tease him by brushing her ass against his hard-on, but she decided to wait and see how much freedom he'd allow her first. He didn't seem to be in any hurry to frisk her, and every second that passed revved her desire up another hot notch. Her body was a live-wire of tingling, melting sensations. What was he thinking?

"Don't move." He positioned her hands against the truck, and kicked her feet apart, arranging Sunny like he wanted her.

She hadn't planned on moving. His hands returned to her shoulders and flexed slightly, revealing the strength of his touch. Then slowly, he began to move his hands down Sunny's arms. The caress-like touch made her breath catch and she closed her eyes so that every one of her senses was engaged in what Officer Steele was making her feel. Circling her wrists, he began the journey up the underside of her arms.

Sunny held her breath when he reached the sides of her breasts, and stopped. She bit down on her lip to keep from voicing her needs. With her luck he'd do just the opposite. His hands moved about an inch, teasing her. The bastard knew what she wanted, damn him! In the next instant she nearly sank to her knees. His large hands had come around to cover her breasts, and it was no light pat.

A whimper escaped Sunny as he squeezed and kneaded her breasts through her blouse. His fingers pinched her already hard nipples roughly, before he took her breasts into his hands as if weighing them. She could hear his breathing escalate against the back of her neck. The knowledge that she was affecting him gave her the courage to arch back far enough to rub her butt against his hard cock.

Sunny was unprepared for his angry reaction. His hands fell to her hips and he pushed her away roughly. "I told you not to move," he reminded her in a gravelly voice. "Do it again and I'll cuff you."

It was no idle threat. Sunny's instincts warned her that Officer Steele didn't say anything he didn't mean. In spite of his warning, his dominance excited her, as long as it didn't go too far. She tried to relax, hard to do considering his hands had returned to her breasts; only he was no longer content to caress her outside her blouse. Taking hold of the fragile material of her blouse, Officer Steele ripped her blouse open at the front, and pulled it halfway down her shoulders.

Sunny moaned loudly, silently encouraging him to do whatever he wanted. She was beyond rational thought, and all he'd done so far was touch her breasts. As his hands glided over the cups of her lacy bra, he discovered the front hook, and it wasn't long before Sunny's naked breasts were in his hands. *Oh, God!* Her panties had to be soaked by now. Everything he did made her hot.

"Is it okay if I ask you what your first name is?" she asked in a smoky voice. His hands roamed down her ribcage, and over her belly.

"Wade," he answered gruffly, reaching the waist of Sunny's shorts. He deftly unsnapped them, and yanked the zipper down. Then his hands flattened against Sunny's lower belly and traveled lower, beneath her shorts and over her panties, to the V between her legs. One long finger flicked over her crotch.

Holy shit! She was going to go up in flames, and she jerked with pleasure. If he punished her then so be it, she couldn't stop her body from responding. His grunt and the rapid breathing behind her told Sunny that Mr. Control was losing it, slowly but gradually.

"Fuck, baby," Wade leaned in and spoke against Sunny's ear. His warm breath sent a shiver of delight down her spine. "You're soaked."

No longer content to tease her pussy through her panties, Wade moved the silk aside easily and touched Sunny's outer pussy lips, before wiggling his finger between the folds to where her clit was located. She let out a small cry, willing him to end it. His unhurried, sensual movements were driving her mad, and she was close to climaxing. As if sensing her need Wade circled her clit several times, nearly bringing Sunny to her knees.

She began to move her hips, uncaring if he liked it or not. Lust was eating her up, and coming would relieve some of the fire in her blood. Whimpers mingled with low groans as Wade manipulated Sunny's clit with urgency. Suddenly she was sandwiched between him and her truck, as he leaned into her and rubbed his cock against her ass. His movements indicated he was aiming for his own pleasure.

Sunny rocked against Wade's finger wildly, so close. She felt her orgasm spiraling through her body toward her cunt, willing it to hurry. Every thrust of her hips brought her closer to heaven. Then, in a lightning fast move, Wade pulled away, turned Sunny around, picked her up and deposited her on the hood of her truck. Before she could comprehend what he was doing he pulled her shorts down her legs and off, along with her flip-flops, and tossed them to the ground.

His expression of raw, animal lust nearly drove Sunny over the edge. She didn't have time to be embarrassed over her vulnerable position. Wade parted her legs with barely controlled roughness, and moved into the V he'd created against the truck. Sunny sucked in her breath as their heated gazes met and clung. He'd left on her panties. Their gazes remained locked when he put his hands on her knees and slowly moved them up her quivering thighs.

"You have a beautiful body, lady." His large hands spanned the crease where Sunny's thighs met with her lower body. His thumbs flicked over her pussy in a teasing manner that tore a moan from her throat. How much more could she take from this man? She had to fight the urge to keep from demanding that he fuck her. "Have you been fucked today?"

What? What kind of a question is that at a crucial moment like this? She stared into his dark eyes, struggling between the truth and fibbing. "I–"

"Don't lie either." *Oh shit!* She heard the mild threat in his tone. Something told Sunny he would know, too. "Has there been a cock in this pretty little cunt today?"

His graphic comment caused a delicious shiver over Sunny. "I have a husband," was all she was willing to admit to.

"A husband, huh?" he grinned. He leaned in close enough to put his nose against her pussy. Inhaling deeply, he closed his eyes as if savoring something good. "Sweet, cunt. I'm going to enjoy eating you out."

Sunny collapsed against the hood, and then nearly jumped off when she felt Wade's tongue run over the seam where her pussy lips met. She arched wildly, crying out. "Wade!" she couldn't help calling out.

His fingers curled around the narrow strip of silk between her legs and without warning he ripped the fragile material away. Sunny was completely naked from the waist down now, and in the most vulnerable position she'd ever been in before. She lifted her head enough to meet Wade's eyes. His wink surprised her.

"Time to get down to business."

Chapter 4

Sunny soon found what business Wade was talking about. She let out a shriek when he pulled her closer to the edge of the hood. The next thing she knew his head was between her legs and his tongue was buried deep inside her pussy. She sighed in total bliss, as he did exactly what he'd said he was going to do. He used every part of his talented mouth to explore, and pleasure every part of Sunny's cunt. She closed her eyes, preparing to explode with pleasure.

It didn't take long for Sunny to peak. Wade was very good at taking things slow and easy, while stroking the embers that were going to consume her. She felt her orgasm racing for the finish line, and he seemed to sense it. His tongue action picked up speed, jabbing into the depths of her pussy as deep as it could go, touching, lapping, and sucking. He replaced his tongue with his fingers, locating her G-spot, so he could focus on her throbbing clit with his mouth.

"Wade!" Sunny cried out, convulsing with the intense force of her orgasm. He wrapped his hands around her upper thighs and held her in place, continuing to use his tongue on her, long after the waves of release wound down to the occasional tremor.

Sunny was too weak to move. Wade had no such trouble...making her move. He grabbed the opened ends of her ruined blouse and pulled her up into a sitting position. A cry escaped her when she realized she was beginning to slip off the hood, but he moved in and she was suddenly flush against the handsome cop. Her hands automatically came down on his shoulders for support, her eyes rounding with surprise when she saw the seriousness of his expression.

Glancing down, Sunny wasn't disappointed. Wade was still hard. In fact, she was amazed that his zipper was containing such a huge muscle.

She was eager to see to his needs, still hoping she was going to get out of those tickets. The first thing in order was wiping that much too serious expression off his face.

Sunny smiled enticingly, leaning in to kiss him, wondering if he'd let her. Moving in slow motion gave him plenty of time to convey his feelings. The closer she got to his masculine mouth the more she wanted to taste him.

Suddenly Wade grabbed Sunny by the upper arms. "Kiss me all ready!" he growled, slanting his mouth down over hers with impatience.

The pressure of his kiss forced her mouth open, and then he was slipping his tongue inside. The texture, warmth and taste of his mouth caused desire to race through Sunny. She knew she was tasting herself on his tongue but didn't care. They explored each other's mouths until they were both out of breath.

Sunny felt a little drunk on Wade. Reaching forward, she ran the tip of her finger down the ridge of his huge cock. It jumped strongly, prompting her to lower the zipper slowly. She stared into his eyes, looking for any sign that warned her to stop. A sound of startled surprise escaped her when the material parted and his cock fell into her hands, literally. The man was hung like a horse!

She looked down. Oh. My. God. A fresh wave of liquid heat flowed to the very core of her. There was no way she could get her mouth on him from her position, so she moved to get down. Wade helped her by putting his hands on her waist, and Sunny slid down his body until her feet were on the ground. A loud moan erupted from her when his stiff cock left a trail of fire where it brushed against her skin. Sunny didn't stop when her feet were on the ground, though, she continued until she was on her knees.

Wade's hands tangled in her hair, forcing her to look up. She could see the clouded desire in his eyes. His expression resembled that of a man consumed with longing. His cock was waving in her face, and

Wade thrust forward so that it rubbed against Sunny's lips. She breathed in his musky scent, nuzzling her nose close to his balls. Sticking her tongue out, she ran the tip along the length of his cock.

"Oh, fuck!" he rasped, slapping his hands on the truck as if for support.

Smiling, Sunny was pleased over his reaction. She teased him some more, exploring the veins and ridges of his thick member with her mouth, until coming to the rounded head. He had so much pre-cum that it had filled the slit and was running over. She eagerly lapped it all up, feeling the quiver ripple through Wade's muscles. He was a big man, and it thrilled her to know she was pleasing him to the point that he was fighting to stay on his feet.

Sensing his patience was running out Sunny finally took his cock into her mouth. Soft velvet over hot steel, she couldn't wait to have him inside her. His hands flexed in her hair, as if he couldn't control himself he thrust forward until he was at the back of her throat.

"Aaaaggghhh!"

Sunny swallowed, knowing from experience that most men loved the feel of throat muscles working their cock head. Wade was no different, groaning low and deep. She glanced up at him long enough to see he'd thrown his head back and ecstasy controlled his expression. His pleasure fueled her need to give him more, and she began to love his sex with one purpose in mind, to make him come.

"Aaaaggghhh! Sweet Jesus!"

When it happened Sunny locked her mouth around his shaft and swallowed everything he had to give. His cum hit the back of her throat, and with moans of pleasure she pumped him until he was dry. She barely finished when Wade grabbed her, hauling her to her feet. Their mouths slammed together in a rough, passion filled kiss that seemed to grow tenderer as time moved on.

"You have a very talented mouth," he said when their lips pulled apart. His hands came up to cup Sunny's breasts, which were still bare.

"Talented enough to get out of those tickets?" She gave his chin a love bite.

Wade pushed her back and glanced down at her full breasts. "Tempting." He dipped his head so he could run his tongue over the nipples. He took his time licking them before meeting her eyes again. "But I told you I was going to fuck you."

Sunny's mouth dropped as his declaration fueled her lust.

"Get in the back of the truck," Wade ordered. As he pushed her in the direction he tore the rest of her blouse off her. The bra slipped away on its own.

When they reached the back of her truck Sunny turned around. "It's getting late and I have to meet my husband."

He didn't blink, just reached around her and let down the tailgate. "Then we'd better hurry."

She glanced around the area, taking in the old, boarded up house, and over grown lawn. No one could see them from the road, which was why she'd pulled in there. Now she was thankful that she had. The cop in front of her began pulling off his equipment and setting it down in the truck off to the side. Next he undid the buttons to his shirt.

When he opened his shirt to take it off Sunny couldn't take her eyes off his torso. *Damn, he's buff!* She reached forward to touch his defined chest, wanting proof he was as hard as he looked. *He is!* She sighed, running her hand over his warm flesh, and then lower, over his abs. Suddenly she couldn't wait to feel him on top of her.

The amusement on his handsome face revealed he knew Sunny liked what she saw. He took his discarded shirt and spread it out on the bed of the truck, then reached for his belt buckle. In seconds his shoes and pants joined the rest of his stuff in the back of the truck. His cock was already stiff again.

A naked Wade Steele took Sunny's breath away, and turned her on faster than nothing else. He had the whole stud package. Everything about him was big and solid. Her caress took her lower, but before she could claim her prize Wade grabbed her by the wrist and stopped her. She looked at him questioningly. He transferred his hands to her waist and picked her up, depositing her in the back of the truck, and joining her with ease.

As he continued down and over Sunny she found herself flat on her back. Wade settled his weight on top of her, wedging his cock tightly between her legs. She caught her breath, whimpering with anticipation as his hot member slid along the seam of her pussy lips. He moved purposely against her mound, ran his hands up the sides of her body and caressed her breasts. His kiss was rough with growing passion, igniting hers.

She squirmed beneath Wade, moving her hands over his shoulders, back and tight buttocks, eager for him to fuck her. His cock twitched when she squeezed the hard moons of his ass. God, she wanted him inside her. *What's he waiting for?*

"Fuck me, damn you!" she exploded, losing impatience. She arched beneath him, which caused his cock to slip between her pussy lips and rub against her labia. "I need you," she whispered, trembling with hunger.

His low chuckle wasn't what she'd been expecting, but in the next instant he took hold of his member and poised it at her entrance. Sunny braced herself, Wade was a big man. He took her mind off his imposing size when he rubbed the head of his cock up and down her slit. Every time he hit her clit she arched with reaction.

"You're so responsive." He leaned down and tongued her nipple. "Think you can handle this?" By *this* he meant his cock. He thrust in a couple inches and then pulled out. Sunny nodded eagerly, barely breathing. "Okay, baby, on the count of three." He locked eye contact with her. "Ready?"

Sunny nodded.

"One." Wade thrust forward, burying himself to the hilt. "Aaaaagggghhhh!" he grunted.

He'd tricked her! Sunny cried out in pleasure, bowing her body sharply beneath his as his cock slid into her cunt in one long, delicious stroke. Her low, drawn out groan followed. Wade's large shaft filled her completely, massaging her insides with a solid caress. Before she had time to soak in the exquisite feeling he backed out in slow motion.

"How do you want it?" He spoke the words against her lips.

Sunny was tired of slow. She looked up at him, recognizing the look of intense desire on his face, the glazed eyes, flared nostrils, and taut jaw that seemed to be a universal look in the moment of passion. Her face, she imagined, probably looked the same way to him.

"Fast and hard," she said simply. She barely got the words out when Wade began to move.

As he pumped in and out in a steady rhythm, Sunny ran her hands over his body wherever she could touch him. Sometimes she used her nails like a cat, sharpening them down his back. He punished her by picking up her legs and draping them over his shoulders, and picking up speed. He slammed into Sunny over and over.

"Oh, God, Wade!" she cried, overwhelmed with the pleasure of having his cock glide over her sensitive clit. The new position thrust her pelvis upward giving him the perfect opportunity to slide against her clit on his way down and into her pussy. Seconds later she was consumed by the on-coming rush of another orgasm. "I'm going to come!"

He grabbed Sunny by the hips and began moving so fast that she knew he was getting ready, too. He slammed his mouth down on hers, and grunted. Sunny felt liquid fire burst inside her pussy and realized that he was coming. That knowledge pushed her over and she crashed with him. Clinging to one another, they convulsed uncontrollably.

Chapter 5

"You're a good fuck," Wade said against Sunny's neck, where he'd come to rest. He lifted his head to meet her eyes. "You have a lucky husband."

She smiled. "I'm pretty lucky, too." She ran her hands lightly over his shoulders, before lifting up to give him a brief kiss. "What about those tickets?"

He chuckled, amusement filling his eyes. "I'll let it go with a warning this time," he replied. "But we need to get that taillight fixed. I don't want another cop stopping you, wouldn't look good for me as the new cop in town." She and Wade had only moved back there two months before.

Sunny nodded. "My new tag is in the glove box." She'd picked it up the day before. "Did you bring something home for dinner?"

They both moaned a little as his deflated cock slipped out of her body. "I knew you'd be hungry after we fucked. I picked up some Chinese."

"From Chang's?" she asked with excitement. They made the best homemade spring rolls.

Sunny and Wade had both grown up in the small town of River Rock, they'd met there, and married, and had moved away for what they thought would be a better life. Six years in a busy city had them both yearning to return to home where their family and friends were, a place where it was quiet, and the way of life a little slower. It was only natural when the job for a new cop opened up that Wade applied for it, and the fact that he'd come from there had weighed heavily on the decision to hire him.

Being back home again made Sunny very happy.

"Is there any place else?" he teased, pushing to his feet. He held his hand down to help her to her feet. Once there he pulled her against him. "Happy birthday, honey." He squeezed her ass cheeks.

"Thank you. This was a nice surprise." Sunny was talking about what just happened between them. When discussing their secret fantasies a couple days before, she'd confessed that she'd always wanted to be ravished by a cop, someone with power who she couldn't say no to.

"I was worried you wouldn't realize what I was doing when I pulled you over."

"Not a chance. I knew you were smart when I married you."

He slapped her behind, and then caressed the spot. They stood for a moment, looking at the old country house. "Did the realtor give you the keys yet?"

Sunny nodded happily. "The house is all ours. We can take possession any time." She knew what Wade was thinking as he stared at the hundred-year-old, two-story building. It needed painting, new windows, and landscaping, and that was just the outside. The inside needed a major renovation, but it had a lot of country charm, and they'd bought it at a big reduction.

Dusk was turning the sky dark, and with it the temperature was dropping. The fact they were both standing in the bed of her truck, stark naked, drew a chuckle from her. It was a good thing the house was situated away from the road, and the lawn was overgrown.

"What's so funny?" Wade wanted to know.

"Don't you think we should get dressed?"

He stared at her for a moment before saying, "Hell no." He jumped from the truck and reached up for her, swinging Sunny to the ground. "Let's go inside and christen something in there."

"I don't think so," she began, picking up her discarded clothes. "That's not part of my fantasy." She watched him reach inside his open window, and pull out a bag with Chang's Restaurant on the side.

He looked back at her for a moment, letting his gaze roam down her body. In spite of being hungry, Sunny was instantly encased with heat from the warm promise in Wade's eyes. He'd always been able to turn her on with just a look. He held out his hand. "Come on. We'll go inside and eat, and see what develops."

Sunny followed him. She had no doubts that something in that old house was going to get christened.

THE END

On Fire

Chapter 1

WHEN MY BEST FRIEND Shelly and I arrive home from work each night we head straight to our own rooms. We're lucky in that we have our own private baths. I knew she was getting ready for a hot date, and could tell she was in a hurry. She still had a couple of hours before meeting her current boyfriend Chris, and when she went out she dressed to the hilt, which took hours. Shelly was always on the lookout for her next boyfriend, in case things didn't work out with the one she had.

I shut my bedroom door and threw myself down on the bed. Another lonely night at home, just me, Tootsie, and Mr. Big. I really needed to think about replacing Mr. Big, he was more than just broken in, he was broken up. I laughed, thinking about the tape I had to use to keep the batteries from sliding out. Plus, there was a good sized split in the cyber skin phallus that I supposed made it a little unsanitary, not to mention painful when it tugged at the occasional pubic hair. But it was the closest thing to having a real cock inside me, and I could count on him being there whenever I needed him.

I was pathetic! My mind drifted to our hot neighbor Dean. I must have imagined the blatant interest in his eyes the other day while sun bathing out by the pool. Even now I grew uncomfortably warm thinking about the way his eyes had branded every inch of me. Knowing his gaze was on me I'd reached up to undo the back of my bathing suit top, and then lifted up just enough so he could see my large breasts, minus the nipples.

If he'd truly been interested wouldn't he have made a move? The too quiet hunk hadn't done anything more than toss me a crooked smile and a wave. *Jerk!* He wouldn't know a good piece of ass if it was staring him in the face. I laughed, realizing that if I was that good, I wouldn't be alone now.

Maybe he was just shy or something. Lord, please don't let him be some nerdy bookworm! Why would God waste that dynamite body on a geek? Crap, why was I even worried about it? Except that I was horny as hell and every time I saw him I just wanted to jump his bones. I grabbed my pillow and closed my eyes. I'm glad Shelly seemed to be having some luck with Chris; they'd been going hot for a whole month, almost a milestone where Shelly was concerned.

I sighed, trying not to think about sexy Dean with his muscular torso and his long legs encased in those faded jeans, but it was too hard getting his handsome face, and smoking hot body out of my mind...

"FAITH! FAITH!"

Gradually the pounding on my bedroom door dragged me from the yummy dream I was having. "What?" I mumbled into my pillow before turning onto my back and stretching against the rumpled bedding.

"I just wanted to let you know I'm leaving now."

"Come on in." I tried to keep my eyes open. It wasn't easy because I wanted to return to my feel good dream.

"You were sleeping?" Shelly asked with disbelief as soon as she entered my room. "Why don't you come with us? You might meet someone there."

"No way, I'm too young to become the third wheel. Besides, knowing the way you feel, you'll be dragging Chris back here early." She laughed, but didn't deny it. "And do me a favor; don't tell me if you happen to see Dean there."

She made a tisking sound. "Why don't you just make the first move for goodness sake? He's only two doors down, or are you afraid he'll say no?"

I shrugged, and sat up. "Maybe he has a girlfriend that we don't know about. He's only been here a couple of weeks."

"Well, it's his loss," Shelly said. "But you won't know until you try. How do I look?"

"As breath-taking as usual." She did. Shelly, in my opinion, was model material.

"Most likely Chris will be coming home with me tonight." Shelly winked. "Try to be quiet with Mr. Big."

A chuckle burst from me. "Bitch!" I knew that was impossible, the whole building had to know when I was having an orgasm. Thank God there were two of us living there so they couldn't possibly know which one of us was wailing like a banshee on her last breath. Okay, maybe I was exaggerating just a little. All I knew was that I sounded loud to me. "Have a good time, honey."

"What are your plans?"

"The usual. Shower, dinner, and a movie." She raised a knowing brow and waited, causing me to break into a reluctant smile.

I shrugged. "Mr. Big."

"That's my girl! Okay, see ya later."

I waved her off, getting to my feet. Time for that shower. I stripped my clothes off as I went, letting them fall to the floor, and flipped on the radio that was sitting on the back of the toilet. By the time I turned on the shower I was naked. Once the water was adjusted to the way I liked it I stepped inside and pulled the curtain closed.

I liked long showers. Besides, with the length and thickness of my hair it took a while to make sure all the shampoo was out. I was at the tail end of rinsing off when I thought I heard a sound above the loud song playing on the radio. I pulled the curtain back and listened for a second, deciding it was nothing, and went back to rinsing off. I started to sing along to Shout it Out Loud when a deafening, sonic-type boom rattled through the whole apartment building. I nearly jumped out of my skin, and reached for the tap to turn off the water.

What the hell?

I heard a muffled sound outside my bathroom, was someone actually pounding on the door? I thought Shelly had left, soon realizing that it wasn't her voice.

"Faith! Open the door!"

Before I could think to respond the door crashed in and slammed against the wall. I screamed, and peered around the shower curtain, afraid of what I was going to see. My eyes fell on Dean, standing in the threshold in nothing but a pair of unsnapped, low hanging jeans. I know my mouth dropped, and my gaze was automatically drawn to the opened V like a magnet. Some part of my stunned brain acknowledged that he'd kicked the door in.

I had a habit of locking my bathroom door when I knew I was alone in the apartment. Especially after watching too many Syfy movies, where a lot of bad things seemed to happen in the bathroom, especially in the shower. I also had a vivid imagination.

"What–"

"There's a fire in your kitchen! You need to get out now!"

"Fire?" I repeated dumbfounded. I was trying to wrap my head around what he was saying, glancing past him to see black smoke drifting into my bedroom.

"You need to come with me now!" His voice was laced with heavy impatience. "The fire department is on their way."

I was still hiding behind the curtain. "There's no way I'm going anywhere with you naked! I–"

I didn't get to finish. His face turned red and he said something about not having time for this. He grabbed my hand and yanked me out of the tub. As soon as my foot hit the floor my leg shot out from under me. I would have gone down if it hadn't been for Dean's rock hard body stopping my fall. I let out a cry, he swore some more, and in a heartbeat my breasts were smashed against his chest. I was instantly engulfed in a smoldering heat of lust as my momentum pushed him backwards into the wall.

"Fuck!" He hit it with jarring contact. Our faces were close, we were both breathing heavily but for different reasons. I was very aware my nipples were hardening against his warm skin. "Not very good timing," he finally said, looking down at me with amusement in his eyes.

I didn't pretend not to know what he was talking about. Now was my time to reveal I was just as interested. "Maybe some other time?" His mouth twitched with a slight smile and he nodded, then pushed away from the wall, and I was forced to step away from him. "I'm still not going anywhere with you naked." I could hear the fire alarm ringing from out in the hallway and knew there would be other tenants evacuating the building.

The next thing I knew he ripped the shower curtain off the hooks, folded it around my body a few times, bent, and threw me over his shoulder. I squealed, feeling myself slipping as he stood. "I'm falling!" I tried to wiggle my arms free but he'd wrapped me up like a cocoon.

"Hold on!" He managed to bounce me back into position, and wrap his arms around my upper thighs. I felt my face flush, ever conscious of my size fourteen curves, although he didn't seem to mind. I thanked God the shower curtain was red and not clear because my ass was close to his face.

"I can walk damnit!"

He ignored me, and turned quickly to walk into my bedroom, through the smoke filled apartment, and toward the opened front door. We were almost there when I remembered Tootsie.

"Wait my cat!" I began to squirm.

"My first priority if getting you out of here."

His first priority? I was more confused than ever. "But she won't come to you!"

We reached the door just as three firemen burst into the apartment. I glanced up from my undignified position long enough to take in that they were dressed in full uniform and weighted down by the various tools of their trade. One of them smiled at me and I lowered my head with a groan.

"What have we got?" One of them asked.

"Looks like an electrical, check the stove," Dean replied, surprising me. "The fire is contained in the kitchen right now." He moved around them and headed down the hallway. "Far as I can tell this is the only apartment affected."

"What's up with the fireman's carry?" Another fireman yelled out as we moved down the hallway. I could hear the amusement in his tone.

"Uncooperative female," Dean responded, receiving loud guffaws in return.

"Dean!" I wanted to die of embarrassment. I could hear the shuffling and mumbling of my neighbors as they vacated their apartments and headed toward the stairs. "Where are you taking me?"

"Some place safe for the time being. Until we get your apartment fire under control and assess the damage." He came to a door and opened it.

We? "Are you a fireman?"

"Yes ma'am." He set me down on my feet. "I was returning from the mailbox when I noticed smoke coming out from beneath your door. I pulled the alarm and the rest you know." He turned to leave.

"Wait a minute! You can't leave me like this."

His gaze moved down my curtain clad body. The only thing visible was my neck and wet head. If he left me and I fell to the floor I'd lay there like a helpless slug until his return. The corners of his mouth lifted, as if he was thinking something similar.

"I guess it won't hurt to turn you loose."

He located the ends of the plastic and slowly spun me around as if I was a ballerina on top of a music box. Every turn left him with more curtain in his hands until I was standing completely naked before him...*again.*

Cool air touched my damp, exposed skin, but it was the hot interested look in Dean's eyes that made me shiver. I ran my gaze with deliberately slowness over his chest, arms and abs, pausing at where his jeans were slightly open. *God, he makes me hungry!* Remembering what it had felt like when my breasts were crushed against him didn't help. When I raised my gaze to his, I realized he was looking me over just as thoroughly.

I waited until his gaze met mine again before saying, "Please don't forget my pussy when you go back." I knew it was an outrageous thing to say, but I was rewarded when his pupils dilated. Fire exploded in my blood because that one tiny change, that he couldn't control, told me he was turned-on. "Her name is Tootsie."

He didn't miss a beat. "Big white cat?" he asked.

He must have seen her in the window because she was an inside cat. "Yes."

"Okay, I gotta get back. Feel free to look for something to wear from my closet." He turned, and closed the door behind him.

I stood there for a moment, looking around his masculine, neat apartment. Well, at least I was naked, and in his apartment. All I had to do now was get him into bed.

Something told me that was going to be easy.

Chapter 2

As I wandered toward a doorway that I was certain led to Dean's bedroom I realized that I needed to call Shelly and tell her what happened. I was pretty sure neither of us would be able to spend the night in our apartment. Even if it was deemed safe to return by the fire department, the smell of smoke might be overwhelming, and whatever damages would have to be repaired by management. Going from past experiences, it could be a while.

Dean's bedroom was as masculine as the man. I had to admit he had good taste, taking in the quality of the furniture, and art that decorated his walls. It looked like he wasn't afraid to invest good money on quality. My gaze went to his oversized bed, and I couldn't help imagining us laying there, naked and fucking our brains out.

I opened the closet door, and stood back, letting my gaze roam over the contents. A row of shirts caught my eye and I reached for the first one I saw. It was a pullover and I slipped it on, pulling it down over my ass. A glance in his mirror revealed it barely covered my privates, stopping at the top of my thighs. Not bad. The green color complimented my hazel eyes, and the soft material clung to my curves. I fluffed up my damp hair, going for that sultry bedroom look.

A sound coming from the outer room had me leaving the bedroom to investigate. I halted upon seeing that Dean had returned, smiling when I noticed how he was holding Tootsie away from his body.

"You're back," I said unnecessarily.

He deposited my cat on the floor. "Your cat has claws."

There were several rows of scratches lining the top-half of his chest, over the area of his heart. "Oh, my!" I said. "Where's your first aid kit?" I was eager to play nurse, anything to get my hands on him.

"That's okay." He brushed it off. "I need to get back."

He turned but before he could take a step the door was pushed open and a fireman stepped into the room. "Fire's out." His interested gaze shifted from Dean to where I was standing. He gave me a quick and impersonal once over before looking back at Dean. "Looks like you were right about the oven. The wiring isn't up to code."

"I wonder how many other units is the same way," Dean said.

The fireman shrugged. "There will have to be an investigation." This time when he glanced at me he didn't look away. "You can return for some of your things but you won't be able to stay until the investigation is complete. Maintenance will need to repair the damage, too. Do you have some place to go?"

His friendly expression and the tone of his voice gave me the feeling that he was going to make an offer if I said the right thing. I smiled at him in return, and opened my mouth to let him know that I had friends I could call.

"She has some place to go," Dean said before I could get out a word. The look he and his friend exchanged spoke volumes between them. I wasn't a dummy. It suddenly occurred to me that the fireman was purposely baiting Dean, as if he knew something I didn't. *Interesting.*

"Just thought I'd ask," the fireman said with a grin. "See you around buddy." He gave Dean a friendly pat on the arm and then he was gone.

I met Dean's eyes. "How do you know that I have some place to go?" Crossing my arms probably wasn't the smartest move because I could feel my borrowed shirt inch up my body. It didn't make me adjust my stance and I was glad I didn't when Dean closed and locked his door before turning back to me with what seemed like deliberate slowness.

There was amusement in his eyes. "Because you're already there," he said with confidence.

Well, this was new! I wanted to ask him if he was the same guy at the pool the other day. The same one who'd looked me over with interest before walking away. Maybe he had a twin? No, there couldn't be two drop dead gorgeous hunks with the same tattoo of an eagle in flight on his bicep.

"Is this an invitation to stay here?" I didn't want there to be any misunderstandings between us.

"If you want."

"I didn't think you were interested."

He looked surprised, and then grinned that crooked sexy grin that took my breath away. "Oh, I'm interested." He started to walk toward me. "I've been interested in you since the first time I saw you bent over unloading groceries from your car. Your cute ass stopped me dead in my tracks."

Cute ass? A shiver of delight ran over me. "How come you never said anything?" He stopped directly in front of me. I had to glance up a long way to look into his smiling, brown eyes.

"Several reasons," he said. "But mostly the timing never seemed right. I wanted to make sure when I finally made my move that we had time to take things slow and easy."

In spite of being hornier than hell and wanting nothing more than for him to fuck my brains out fast and furious, I liked the sound of that. I finally gave in to the impulse to touch him, placing my palm against his hard chest. "I've been wanting to touch you."

He laughed. "If you only knew what I've been wanting to do to you. Wet dreams are a bitch."

God, he knew just what to say to drive my desire up a notch. I couldn't help visualizing him walking up after having an orgasm with me on his mind. "Why don't you show me what you'd like to do?" I watched a muscle twitch in his lean jaw as I moved my hand over him softly. "I think we've probably been wanting the same thing." I silently marveled at how freakin' muscled he was. As my caress took me down his torso to where the opening of his jeans was, Dean sucked in a deep breath. I smiled, noticing movement where I wanted my hand to be.

Did I dare? I so wanted to slide inside his pants and check out the size of his cock. Just thinking about it produced a warm, wet feeling between my legs. I searched his eyes for encouragement, and lowered my hand inch by inch. Right before I got to my prize Dean reached forward and caught me around the wrist to halt my progress.

"I like it slow and easy, remember?"

I swallowed, as my breathing picked up speed, wondering what I could do to make him change his mind. *Is he testing me?* Slow and easy was nice, but I hadn't been with a man in a few months and I was hungry. I wanted to consume Dean, until the ache inside had been satisfied. Maybe I should just come out and tell him how I feel.

"Slow and easy is nice for the second round," I began, pulling my wrist gently from his grasp. "But I've been horny for you since you moved in. That's a lot of sexual frustration stored up." I was surprised he didn't stop me a second time as I slid my hand downward beneath his jeans. The closer I got to his cock, the hotter his flesh felt, the coarser the hair. I closed my eyes and moaned when I completed my journey.

Dean groaned, his body rippling with reaction. I opened my eyes to find that his were closed, and his expression was taut with raw desire. I felt empowered, closing my hand around a hot, sizable muscle. Soft satin covering solid steel. I found his cock thick and long and not lacking in any way. I squeezed until he emitted another low groan. Hoping to speed things along, I leaned forward and tongued his firm nipple.

"Holy fuck!"

His eyes flew open and I knew he'd gone from zero to a hundred in five seconds flat. Slow and easy wasn't revealed on his handsome face. Need and lust burned bright in his eyes. God, I wanted him to kiss me and raised my face, offering him the opportunity to swoop down and do it. He didn't disappoint me. Before I knew it Dean wrapped an arm around my waist, jerked me against him and covered my mouth with his.

The man knew how to kiss! It was everything a first kiss should be. His lips were smooth and firm, working over mine like a slow, thorough caress. I opened my mouth beneath the gentle persuasion of his, letting his tongue push inside to mingle with mine, before we moved on to explore the texture, warmth and softness of each other's mouths. Mutual moans of pleasure surrounded us, and I was engulfed in a melting heat when Dean's hands smoothed down my backside to my butt. Feeling his hands caressing my naked flesh was the catalyst of immeasurable things to come.

His growing passion fueled mine, and I began to stroke his magnificent cock with more vigor. Then, with impatience because of the constriction of his jeans, I pulled my hand out to finish unzipping his pants. Just as quickly my hands went to the V created by the lowering of his zipper, and I easily moved his jeans out of the way with a well placed caress. Dean's shaft popped free into my waiting hands, and for the first time I was able to see how really massive his cock was.

Sweet Jesus, he was going to stuff me and then some and I couldn't wait. Since his hands were still on my ass I brought mine around to his and held him to me while I arched my bare pussy against his rod. We both expelled loud sounds of appreciation at the exquisite feeling of flesh against flesh, but it was lust that drove us to the next move. Before I could brace myself Dean picked me up and deposited me on the kitchen counter. Breathing out of control, we looked into each other's eyes. Words seemed unnecessary as we both knew we'd reached the point of no return. In the next moment he pulled me to the edge of the counter and onto his waiting cock.

I threw my head back and howled. Not because it hurt, but from the intense pleasure when he penetrated my pussy all the way to the hilt. *Oh, God!* I wrapped my legs around his waist, pulling him even tighter against me. Dean grunted, and then his whole body shuddered. He slammed his mouth down over mine, and began to move his hips, slow and easy. I smiled against his lips.

He pulled back, but continued thrusting.

"Faster, Dean," I coaxed, biting down on his bottom lip.

"I like it slow."

"Harder," I said, reaching up to tweak his nipple.

"I like it easy."

"Next time," I reminded him, raking my nails down his back.

He bowed but didn't pick up speed. It was pain and pleasure. His steady pace was giving me time to fully appreciate the full thickness of his dick, while slowly driving me insane. Most of the guys I'd been with were the slam bam thank you ma'am types. Into it for a quick, satisfying fuck that left me on the losing end of the stick. Dean wasn't fucking me like a man who only wanted one thing. He was taking his time and making sure that my ecstasy equaled his.

"Dean," I couldn't remember the last man who'd made me feel what I was feeling right then. "This feels so good!"

"It's supposed to," he smiled.

His hands were on my hips. Suddenly they were taking the hem of the shirt I was wearing and he pulled it up and over my head. His bright gaze went to my breasts, and then his hands were cupping them, his thumbs flicking over my nipples. I sighed and quivered, then arched forward when he bent to take a peaked kernel into his mouth.

"Beautiful," he said, pulling and nibbling on the nub and watching it swell and turn even harder. He repeated the action on my other nipple, causing me to squirm with pleasant reaction.

While he took his time loving my breasts he stopped thrusting, leaving his cock to rest inside me. There was no way to describe how good it felt as it twitched and pulsed against my insides. I squeezed my muscles, getting a low groan from Dean, and was rewarded when he pulled out and slammed forward again.

"Aaagghh!" I trembled. "Do that again," I panted.

He glanced up from the nipple in his mouth, gave it a final lick and pulled his cock out all the way. "I have a better idea," he said as he began to kiss his way down my body.

I held my breath as he neared my sex, my thighs quivering on either side of his head. God I was glad I'd just had a shower. In spite of that, the heady scent reaching my nose revealed we were both highly aroused, as sex had an aroma like nothing else. My ass nearly left the counter when I felt Dean's hot breath against the top of my pelvic bone.

"Oh!"

"Easy, baby." His hands took firm hold on my fleshy thighs.

If he hadn't been pinning me in place, I would have slid to the floor in a puddle of mindless mush when his tongue traced the seam of my pussy in teasing sweeps. I clenched my hands into his shoulders, and threw my head back in sheer bliss. My juices were flowing freely, I could feel a tickling wetness run between the crack of my butt. I was so close to an orgasm that I was afraid of losing control.

"Dean–aaagghh!" All thoughts left my head when his warm tongue burrowed between my pussy lips, glided past my labia, and wiggled into my buzzing channel. The way his mouth was locked onto my sex, his upper lip caressed my sensitive clit. Oh sweet heavens the man knew how to work his mouth and tongue on a cunt. My breath catching, I began to rock my hips against his thrusting tongue.

"Dean!" I cried out, coming almost immediately. I convulsed against his mouth, letting the smooth flow of hot release control my movements.

My hands tangled into his hair, but there was no need. He didn't make any effort to pull away. If anything Dean seemed determined to consume every drop of cum that fell onto his tongue.

Chapter 3

Ibarely caught my breath when Dean rose to his feet and picked me up. I instinctively wrapped my legs around his waist and my arms around his neck, nuzzling my nose against the side of his neck as he walked us to his bedroom. "That was worth waiting for," I breathed into his ear, very conscious of my naked breasts against his chest.

"I'm glad you think so," he replied, lowering us down onto his bed. He kissed me passionately, running his hands up my sides to my breasts. I could feel his hard cock slide naturally between my legs, teasing the entrance to my sex with brushes of heat.

I turned my head, breaking the kiss. "I want you inside me," I whispered, arching my hips. "Fuck me, Dean, *please*!" If I sounded desperate, I didn't care. I reached between our bodies with the intention of taking control of the moment when he surprised me by grabbing my wrist.

He yanked my arm up over my head and pinned it down on the bed. Then did the same thing to the other. I was totally helpless and at his mercy, and could do nothing more than squirm beneath him. After a few seconds I realized I wasn't getting anywhere, and stopped, slightly out of breath. Dean was smiling down at me, totally enjoying his power over me. I moaned and closed my eyes when his cock throbbed strongly against my pussy.

As if to tease me more he took both wrists into one of his hands, and trailed his fingers lightly down my body. The caress turned into a tickle and all I got for my attempt at squirming away was a husky chuckle.

"Ticklish?"

"No," I lied.

Dean reached between us and took his cock in his hand. I was so hungry for him to end my torture that I arched sharply, hoping to impale myself. Laughing, he rubbed my clit gently, causing me to whimper. Round and round he went, using the head of his cock. It didn't matter that I'd already climaxed once, in no time Dean was pulling another one from my hungry, love-starved body. As it spiraled, spiked, and crested he filled my convulsing cunt with one powerful, lunge.

"Aaagghhhhh! You don't play fair!" Multiple orgasms at the same time? I couldn't believe it, and yet, I swear it was happening. No sooner had one orgasm hit me than a second followed, and my constricting muscles were milking his cock.

"Damn," Dean grunted. He shuddered against me.

"That's what you get for teasing me." I managed to get out between pants.

He began thrusting, slow and easy like he liked it.

"I wonder what it would take to make you lose control," I joked.

He looked into my eyes, the beautiful brown in his reminded me of melting chocolate. "You want me to lose control?"

Did I? I had to admit Dean's slow and easy technique was intensely pleasurable. A welcome change from a guy who couldn't take the time to enjoy his partner, me, by making sure he saw to my needs, too. Dean was the opposite of what I was used to, and it occurred to me that I'd been hanging out with the wrong kind of men.

As he continued to thrust I was astonished to realize another orgasm was building. Each time he raised his hips and thrust downward, directly over my aching clit. The pleasure was almost more than I could bear. I let my hands travel over his shoulders, and down his back, feeling his muscles flex beneath my caress. Dean was in prime condition, everything hard and tight, including his butt. My exploration took me over those enticing moons, down the backs of his thick thighs, and back up again.

"I like touching you," I admitted out loud. I turned my face and licked his neck. "I like tasting you." I bowed my hips to meet his every thrust. "I like having your cock deep inside me." He grunted. I bit down gently on his shoulder. He grunted some more. I smiled. "I've never had sex with a man who's given me four orgasms."

He pulled back and our eyes met. "Four?"

"Yes!" I hissed, feeling another one roll through my body in one, long, and sensuous wave. I was helpless against it as it consumed by whole being, my soul. "Aagghhh!" I cried out, convulsing uncontrollably.

At the most intense moment of my climax Dean began to pick up speed. His well aimed thrusts were designed to give my orgasm longevity, while he sought his own release. He was powerful in his possession. His square-jawed expression was set like stone; the fire in his eyes singed me, his nostrils flaring as he pistoned in and out of my pussy. Soon he was shoving his cock inside me one last time, going as deep as he could, and grunting with his release.

"Oh, fuck, aaagggghhh!"

I closed my eyes, feeling ribbons of cum spray my insides. Dean was still holding my arms pinned above my head, and there was nothing I could do other than enjoy his body grind and shudder against mine. Gradually his movements slowed, and his sounds of gratification silenced into heavy breaths. He released my wrists and slowly collapsed, resting his forehead against mine.

Our eyes met and clung. "I kind of like slow and easy," I teased against his lips.

He smiled against my mouth. "Anyone can do hard and fast." He began rubbing his nose against mine. "Slow and easy gives us time to appreciate what we're exploring and touching, what we're doing to one another. It sharpens our sensations."

I couldn't agree more. I wrapped my arms around his neck and arched my lower body against him, enjoying Dean's weight on me. As his cock diminished in size he gradually slipped out of me, leaving me with a feeling of emptiness that I couldn't begin to understand. I'd finally gotten the man I'd been wanting and dreaming of, and I didn't want it to end. Was it too much to hope for that this was a beginning of something more?

"You're quiet."

I laughed softly. "You should talk. We've been passing each other in the hallway for two weeks and you've barely said a dozen words to me."

Dean pulled back slightly. "I ignored you for a reason," he said, surprising me. "I've been in training since I moved here. I couldn't afford to get involved with anyone until that part of my life was over. I'd already planned on making a move on you when the time was right."

"So, your training is over now?"

He shook his head. "I have three more days, but the fire in your apartment kind of sped things up."

"I'm lucky you happened along when you did. I didn't smell a thing."

He nodded his agreement. "I took the liberty of letting the office know for you. I have a feeling they're in for a big expense with updating the electrical for the complex."

"I need to call Shelly, too."

"Later." Dean rolled to the side, pulling me with him as he went. I ended up on top of him.

His kiss was passionate and toe-curling, and I could feel his cock hardening between my thighs. A little wiggling and I was able to position my pussy directly over it. He groaned deep, and bowed his hips, grinding his hard-on against me. Moaning simultaneously, our mouths slanted one way and then the other, as we tried to consume each other in a wet kiss that turned rough with need.

Dean tangled his fingers into my hair and pulled my head back. Our gazes held, filled with renewed desire, and then he was looking over my face, and down my neck and chest to my breasts. It didn't take much persuasion on his part for me to shift up his body far enough so that he could suck my nipples. As soon as his hot mouth closed over my breast I felt a heavy wetness release in my cunt. My whimper was as much from that delicious feeling to what Dean was doing to me.

"God, you have nice tits," Dean rasped as he deserted one breast to move on to the other. "The other day when I passed you out by the pool, all I could think of on the way to work was what your nipples would taste like. I had to sit in the car until my hard-on went away."

His confession thrilled me. The whole time he was sucking and tonguing my nipples my loins were grinding against his erection. "I've had a few naughty thoughts about you, too," I admitted, pulling my breasts away when I sat up. Desire burned hot in his eyes, as he ran his gaze over my body. When his hands went to my hips I instinctively knew what he wanted. He picked me up without any trouble, and lowered me gently down his cock. We both released sounds of satisfaction.

"Fuck, you're tight."

I began to move, and it occurred to me that I was the one with control at that moment. I rode Dean slowly at first, savoring the fullness inside my body. After this I knew Mr. Big would never be enough to satisfy me again. As I sat back and braced my hands on his thighs for support, his hands played with my breasts. I dropped my head back, knowing my long hair would brush against his balls and upper thighs.

"Holy fucking shit!"

I smiled triumphantly, hearing the weakness in his ragged tone. "You like that?"

"What do you think?" he rasped.

I picked up speed, and smoothed my palms up his torso and defined chest. His nipples were already hard so I leaned forward and tongued them. I moved to sit back when his hand clenched into my hair and he pulled me down for a long wet kiss.

"I could kiss you all night," I admitted when he let me move away.

"That's good because you're not going anywhere tonight."

I liked the sound of that. "I'd like to get to know you better."

He laughed. "Better than this?"

"You know what I mean."

"Aaaaagghhh!" He groaned and closed his eyes when I adjusted my movements and speed. I reached behind me and ran my fingers over his balls. His thighs quivered. I watched the changes that came over his expression, revealing far more than any words.

Ohmygod! It was amazing how much his cock swelled even more while inside me. How hard and hot it felt. Dean reached forward and began to manipulate my clit. I caught my breath, as lust like I'd never known slammed through me and I started to move faster and wilder. After a while nothing else mattered but coming.

"Oh, God, yes! Right there. That's the spot!"

"Come for me, baby," he coaxed, pinching my clit. His hips left the bed as he buried his dick as deep as it would go. "Oh, shit!"

I cried out, squeezing my muscles around his cock as tight as I could. Until he groaned, stiffened, and lost control. I climaxed soon after, and we clung to each other as wave after wave of pleasure engulfed us and finally diminished into tiny ripples.

"Hungry?" Dean asked sometime later.

"Not anymore," I murmured in a satisfied tone.

His laughter was full and hearty. "I meant for food."

Oh. "Starved," I answered.

He rolled out of bed and held out his hand. I grabbed it and let him pull me to my feet. "How about some left over chicken and potato salad?"

I found myself in his arms. "Sounds good to me."

He smiled and kissed me briefly on the lips. "Good. You call Shelly while I fix us a plate." His hands caressed and squeezed my ass. "After that we'll get better acquainted over a bottle of wine."

I *really* liked the sound of that! I was finally where I wanted to be, well, for at least the last two weeks. Dean's confession of why he'd waited before approaching me told me what kind of man he was, and so far I liked everything about him. Neat, clean, focused, a generous lover, I suddenly realized I'd discovered a lot about him in a short time.

"What's wrong?" Dean asked.

I smiled when his cock began to harden against me. Apparently he had a healthy sex drive, too. Nothing to complain about. "I was just thinking I'd like that, too." I playfully bumped my pussy against him. He bumped back, and we both groaned, falling back onto the bed.

We didn't make it to the kitchen until much later.

THE END

Under Cover

Chapter 1

"LOOK! ONE OF THE PALACE guards." The three friends visiting Buckingham Palace halted after Darla's lively comment.

Lucie gave the man, who was dressed impeccably in a scarlet red uniform and a black hat called a bearskin, a thorough once-over. For a palace guard he was impressive in stature and build, not the thin, wiry guard she'd seen pictures of in the tourist brochure. His uniform fit him like a glove and looked as if it had been poured onto him. There was not as much as a wrinkle in it. He stood backbone-straight and was so still that Lucie stared at his chest until the slightest movement indicated that he was in fact a living, breathing man.

She smiled. *A stud.* Her gaze roamed up to his face. What she could see of it revealed a square jawbone, a firm, yet sensual mouth, and a slightly crooked nose that revealed it might have been broken at least once. From where she was standing she couldn't see his eyes, but she could see the thin scar marring his left cheek.

"Someone go up to him and make him smile," Anna suggested half-jokingly.

"Aren't there rules or something against that?" Darla asked.

Anna waved Darla off. "Lucie, you go, you're the adventurous one."

"I'm not going!" she said, holding back. A vision of ending up in jail while on her vacation flashed before her eyes. "I've planned this vacation for three years and visiting London's jailhouse isn't on my itinerary."

"Come on." Anna looked at Darla as if for backup. "They're not going to put you in jail as long as you don't actually touch him."

"How do you know?" Lucie asked, thinking about all the times that she'd been suckered into doing something for the sake of fun.

"I think I read it somewhere."

"You think?" Lucie wasn't so sure she trusted Anna, even though she was one of her very best friends. The three of them had been together since grade school. "Why don't you do it?"

"You know you're the brave one. Besides, I come up with the ideas."

"Which usually land me in hot water."

Darla laughed. "She's right, Anna. Remember last year–"

"Not everything turns to crap," Anna argued, cutting Darla off. She turned back to Lucie. "Well?"

Lucie glanced back at the guard, who was six feet plus tall. He looked as if he'd been carved in stone, almost frightening. Could she get a rise out of him? The few tourists gathered around him weren't really paying him any mind. They were looking at a map. His expression remained solid, almost challenging someone to try and make him crack. Someone directly in front of him broke out in laughter from something someone in their group had said, but the guard remained stone-faced; his lips didn't as much as twitch.

Huh! Lucie knew a challenge when she saw one and she never backed down, unless it was dangerous or could cause more trouble than it was worth. She'd always been competitive by nature, and suddenly she wanted nothing more than to see some kind of reaction out of him from something that *she* did. As her mind searched for what that something could be she kept her gaze trained on him, looking for a weakness.

"Oh! Oh! I can see it in your eyes, you're gonna do it, aren't you?" Anna said with child-like elation. "Go on, do it now while no one is around."

She was right. The tourists had moved on. Lucie looked around to confirm that there was no one else nearby. Did she dare? She wished she'd paid more attention to the article she'd found about Queen Elizabeth's palace guards. The pamphlet was now stuffed somewhere inside Darla's book bag. The only thing she was certain of was that four guards meant the Queen was in residence, two meant that she wasn't. There were only two guards.

The longer she stared at his lifeless expression the more she felt the urge to do something. Really, how much trouble could she get into? Taking a couple of deep breaths for courage, Lucie walked slowly to where the guard was stationed, coming to a stop when she was about a foot away. She could see his eyes now, barely, just beneath his hat. They were the most startling blue she'd ever seen, reminding her of the cobalt blue glassware she collected, and right now they were unblinking and focused straight ahead. He was a handsome man, even with the scar, which only aided in giving him an air of ruggedness and danger, something she would never have associated with a palace guard.

She couldn't help but smile as she purposely took a step closer and positioned herself directly in his line of sight. Still, he didn't so much as blink or lower his gaze to acknowledge her in any way. His beautiful eyes remained frozen on something behind her in the distance.

"Hi, there, handsome." Nothing, which didn't surprise Lucie. If anything it made her more determined to get a reaction out of him, no matter how small. "I didn't realize the palace guards were so, ah, manly." She raised her hand and snapped her fingers in front of his face. He finally blinked, but his gaze remained straight ahead and fixed over Lucie's head. He towered over her five-foot-seven inch frame.

"Made you blink," she said, smiling and turning to Darla and Anna. "He blinked." She began to walk back to them.

"What are you doing?" Anna exclaimed. "He blinked, big deal, he would have had to do that at some time. Go back and make him smile."

Lucie took a resigned breath and flipped around, wondering why she was listening to Anna in the first place. As she took the few steps back to the guard a thought occurred to her—a naughty thought. She'd already seen several tourists try to make him smile with their funny comments and antics, and he hadn't reacted. Maybe trying to make him smile wasn't the way to go. She halted directly in front of him again, this time a few inches closer. She was close enough to catch the subtle scent of his aftershave, making her realize that he could probably smell her perfume.

"My friends want me to make you smile, but I'm thinking that's not going to happen." Lucie looked him up and down with a critical eye, finding no faults. He really was built. "I'm thinking of something else, something sexy." No response. "Something more, ah, basic to get a reaction out of you." She smiled, wishing he'd lower his gaze to her so she'd at least know that he'd heard her.

"Whatever you're doing it's not working!" Darla yelled out. Lucie heard them both laughing behind her.

"Why don't you just crack that sexy mouth into a smile and save yourself a lot of grief," Lucie suggested to the guard. He did have a sexy mouth. When there was no reaction she shrugged and accepted the silent challenge. "Don't say I didn't warn you big boy, because I don't play fair. I play to win." She took a step closer.

"Now, I know I'm not allowed to touch you, but I have a confession," Lucie purposely lowered her voice. "I *want* to touch you, *all over*. I can tell you have a nice body. I bet you're all hard and tight, and full of mouth-watering muscles." Her gaze fell on his cheek. "The scar on your cheek makes you look hot and dangerous, I wonder if you have anymore, somewhere on your body." She reached up and undid a couple of buttons over her breast. "Whew! I'm getting warm just thinking about how you look without your clothes on, and how warm you'd feel beneath my hands."

Lucie closed her eyes and gently pulled her blouse away from her full breasts, fluffing it as if she was hot. "Maybe while I'm running my hands all over you, exploring the muscles of your chest and abs, and lower, you could put your hands on me. That is, if you'd like to touch me, too. I like having my breasts caressed and my nipples pinched. That *always* get my juices flowing," she hesitated before adding, "I like the feel of a man's wet tongue on them."

She opened her eyes, expecting to see a reaction, and was disappointed when she didn't. "Are you a breast man? Or maybe you're an ass man. Oh!" Lucie whimpered low and gave a little shudder. "Just thinking about your big hands on my ass is turning me on. Especially while you're..." she paused, did she dare? Deciding the odds were against ever seeing him again, she continued in a whisper, "slipping your nice, hard cock inside me." *Crap!* Hearing the words outloud sounded a thousand times more brazen than when it was just a thought in her head. She blamed going too far on knowing that he wouldn't touch her.

When his gaze dropped to hers Lucie caught her breath from the impact of meeting his eyes for the first time. The intensity in those crystal blue orbs sent a shiver of sharp awareness down her spine. He was looking *at* her, not through her, and she had the feeling that the glint turning his eyes almost black carried a warning of some kind. They mesmerized her, not from fear but from the unexpected excitement that zinged through her. She swallowed, caught up in an erotic situation of her own making, too caught up to just walk away.

Damn, I'm actually trembling! She should have left well enough alone, but Lucie wanted more than just a flicker of his eyes. She wanted to know if her words were turning him on. Her curiosity caused her to lower her gaze, but his over-sized coat hid any evidence of a possible erection. Well, there were other subtle signs to look for. She raised her gaze back to his.

"It's too bad we're in a public place and not back at The Stafford London," she glanced around to make sure no one other than Darla and Anna were close by. "I'd love to take off my blouse and rub my naked breasts all over you. God, can't you just imagine my hard nipples scraping against your chest? Delicious!"

Ohmygod! That did it. She saw the first hint that her words had registered with him. His mouth became a pressed line and there was no denying the muscle twitching in his clenched jaw or his flaring nostrils. *Crap, maybe I've gone too far.* She hadn't meant to get so personal, but her desire to some kind of a reaction out of him had taken control of her common sense. Lucie was known for saying what she wanted, but not to complete strangers. She saw his gaze drop to her breasts for a second before lifting to her eyes again. The tiniest flicker on his lips indicated his urge to smile. It happened so fast that at first she thought she'd imagined it.

Did he like what he saw? Glancing down, she groaned inwardly. Her blouse was open and she was exposing more of herself than she'd intended. Her breasts were barely contained in her lacy bra, spilling over the top with every exaggerated breath. Gasping with embarrassment, she quickly turned back to her friends. His reaction to her teasing was so minuscule that they'd never acknowledge it, but she didn't care. Intuition warned Lucie that she'd crossed the line and the only thing saving her from retaliation was his professionalism.

What made it worse was that she'd managed to turn herself on during the process, and had a feeling the guard knew it. She walked back to her friends, ignored their open-mouthed, round-eyed stares, and kept on going. Maybe they *had* noticed.

Too embarrassed for words, Lucie walked all the way back to their hotel without uttering a single word.

Chapter 2

"Are you going to join us down at the bar or not?"

Lucie opened one eye to see Darla standing above her. She was wearing a sexy black dress that was cut into a long V down the front, revealing her almost non-existent breasts. Lucie struggled to hold back her smile, knowing how sensitive Darla was about her lack of feminine assets. In spite of that, her friend looked stunning.

"I'll be down a little later. Did Anna already leave?"

"Yeah, she's meeting the guy we met in the park yesterday."

"They did seem to hit it off."

"Have you ever known Anna *not* to hit it off with a man?" Darla laughed. "Anyway, he promised to bring us some friends."

"Great," Lucie said with little enthusiasm. "You go on down and I'll get ready."

"We'll be inside The American Bar."

As soon as Darla left Lucie sat up and put her feet on the floor. She stretched with a loud groan, feeling refreshed from her power nap. They'd crammed a lot of sightseeing and shopping into their first four days. The three of them had come to a mutual decision that if they were going to enjoy another late evening, they'd better rest up. Now that they'd made a few friends, that night promised to be more than just drinks and shared conversation between them.

She walked barefoot and nearly naked to the closet, taking out the new dress she'd purchased at a little shop not far from the hotel. It was short, tight, and outlined Lucie's curvaceous body to the max, and she'd splurged on it knowing that it would draw attention to her. Red and sexy, she would look smoking in the matching heels she'd purchased, with her blonde hair piled up loosely.

Almost an hour had passed by the time she made it down to The American Bar. She tried not to be self-conscious of her too short dress as it had the desired effect she'd been aiming for. Almost every male in the vicinity ogled her when she walked by, and it didn't seem to matter if they were with someone or not. Lucie knew that she was pretty, she didn't need validation, but every woman enjoyed getting attention when she knew she was at her best.

She walked into The American Bar to see that it was as packed as usual, and she was willing to bet not all of the patrons were tourists or hotel guests. She'd found the English friendly and accommodating, a breath of fresh air. A high pitched whistle drew her attention to a table where three men were drinking. Her gaze touched briefly on each occupant at the table before moving on to find her friends, only to dart back to one man in the group in particular.

Oh crap! He looked so different out of uniform, but she'd recognize those steely blue eyes anywhere. He was looking at Lucie with intensity, narrowing his gaze as he made a laze sweep of her body. Did he recognize her? She watched him pick up his whiskey glass and down the contents in one swallow before slamming the glass on the table with a loud sound, keeping his interest on her the whole time. Warmth engulfed her senses and she felt her cheeks turn hot, but when he said something to his friends and began to scoot out of the booth Lucie quickly turned to go back the way she'd come.

"Lucie, we're over here!"

She glanced over to see Anna waving at her from a corner table. She took in the three men at the table with her friends, only recognizing Seth, the one they'd met at Green Park the day before. Lucie waved back. "I forgot something, I'll be right back!" She didn't even slow down, consciously aware of the man bearing down on her out of the corner of her eye.

She was nearly running when she reached the elevator and punched the button. "*Come on! Come on!*" she mumbled beneath her breath. *Oh thank God!* She felt elation when the doors began to close but before they connected a large hand appeared from nowhere. She caught her breath, her eyes rounding as the doors slowly opened, revealing the man she was trying to avoid. Even out of uniform he was large, and the clothes he was wearing now, a black pull over sweater beneath a black jacket and pants, revealed how truly muscular he was.

As he stepped inside Lucie took a step to go around him. "Excuse me." Her intentions were to slip out, but he purposely blocked her with his body.

Then his hand was on her arm, light enough not to hurt but firm enough to show her he was serious. "I think you and I have some unfinished business to take care of."

The first thing Lucie acknowledged was that his English accent was very faint, while his tone of voice was deep and raspy, sexy sounding. The second thing was that he couldn't be serious! Until then she'd avoided his eyes but now that the elevator door was shut and she was alone with him she reluctantly looked up. Lord, he was handsome! His reddish brown hair was cut close to his head. The scar across his cheek actually added to his appeal, making him look dangerous and capable of anything.

It occurred to Lucie that they weren't moving. She pulled her arm away, hit 4, and moved to the farthest side of the too small elevator. "I don't know what you're talking about." She crossed her arms and gave him her best defiant look. "You must have me confused with someone else." He didn't look at all worried. In fact, he took a step closer. Lucie swallowed nervously, feeling overwhelmed by his sheer size, and, if she was being honest, a little turned on by the look burning in his eyes.

"Oh, don't you." He took another step closer, letting his gaze once again roam with unhurried ease down her body and back up again. "You think I don't recognize you?" He leaned in threateningly. "I recognize your pretty green eyes." Lucie tried to shrink away when he reached toward her. The next thing she knew his hand was tearing the clip holding up her long hair. "I don't see hair this color very often." He picked up a lock and brought it to his nose. "I recognize your scent."

Lucie tried to ignore the flutter of desire uncurling in her belly, and was that her breathing growing heavy? She couldn't tear her eyes from the smoldering, dark fire in his. Something was happening to her. She was afraid of herself more than him. Suddenly she wanted the man crowding her in the elevator. Who would have thought a palace guard could be so hot?

"Your antics left me hard as stone two days ago, and I've been hard ever since. I think it's only fair that you deliver on your promises and put me out of my misery."

Lucie shook her head. "You can't be serious!" she said in a half-whisper. "It was just for fun. Maybe I did go too far but—"

To her surprise he reached behind him and hit a button that stopped the elevator. Then he pushed Lucie up against the wall and pinned her there, moving his face in close. "This is just for fun, too." He slanted his mouth over hers, not giving her a chance to protest. She stiffened and tried to push him away but he easily took hold of her wrists and brought her arms up on either side of her head, pinning them firmly against the wall. She whimpered beneath the attack of his mouth because the almost angry action caused his body to flatten intimately against hers.

She opened her mouth, but he took advantage and slipped his tongue inside, the sudden intimacy acting like a light switch, turning them both wild. Suddenly Lucie was kissing him back, thrusting her tongue against his, moaning with pleasure as she strained into him. His hands slowly uncurled from around her wrists and when Lucie realized she was free she lowered her arms, clenching her hands into the material of his jacket.

The elevator was filled with their sounds of pleasure and heavy breathing as they tried to consume each other. When was the last time she'd been kissed with so much passion by a man who seemed to really be into her? His kiss was thorough, potent, drawing on her hunger as much as feeding it. What had started out almost in anger had run the gauntlet of other emotions that frightened Lucie. It occurred to her that she didn't stand a chance against this man if he should decide to take things further.

As he continued to work his mouth against hers, she thrust her lower body into his. *Ohmygod!* She would have been disappointed to discover that he wasn't hard, but the monstrous size of his rigid cock took her by surprise and drove her lust for him higher. Just the thought of having that long, thick dick inside her made her panties wet. She moaned, letting her hand glide down his body until she reached his erection. She hesitated, should she?

Yes!

Touching him through his pants was like striking a match and watching the flame come to life. His low groan told her how much he liked her hand on him, and the next thing she knew his hands were covering her breasts and squeezing. She whimpered with pleasure as he tweaked her nipples until they were hard, and lightning zigzagged through her body. It didn't seem to matter that they were in a public elevator. All rational thoughts had escaped her as she gave in to his rough, unspoken demands.

Suddenly his hands were smoothing around to her back and down over her rump to where her dress ended. Hands on the back of her thighs, he slowly moved upward in an intimate caress that took him beneath the material to the naked moons of her butt. The breath hissed through his teeth as he squeezed her soft flesh and pulled her even closer to his erection. A volcano erupted inside Lucie in anticipation of fucking this man; because she had no doubt that it was going to end that way.

Their eyes clashed, leaving Lucie to wonder if the shine of lust in his was a reflection of her own. She couldn't recall ever being so turned on before, and she'd never considered having sex with a complete stranger.

She should be alarmed, what did she know about him other than that he was a palace guard? The raw lust darkening his features took all concerns and questions away. Lucie could only think of one thing, and that was satisfying the hunger he'd created.

"Unless you'd like me to fuck you right here in this elevator I suggest you take me to your room, and now." The hoarseness of his tone frightened Lucie into thinking that he would do just that.

Now was her time. She could break away and end the madness consuming them. So why did she wordlessly lead him out of the elevator once it reached her floor and to the room she shared with her friends?

Chapter 3

As soon as Lucie slipped the key into the lock she found herself being pushed into the room, the door slamming shut behind them and then the sound of the lock being turned. She turned to confront the man, but before she could get a word out he pushed her back onto the closest bed, following her down. His weight forced her deeper into the mattress, only she didn't mind. His mouth was on hers again as they kissed passionately for several seconds.

The sounds of animal lust flooded the room. Lucie squirmed and twisted beneath her palace guard, silently encouraging him to fuck her and put her out of her misery. As if reading her thoughts his hands smoothed up her thighs, pushing her dress along as he went. She couldn't stop a small cry when his thumbs brushed over her mound in a teasing sweep before he tore the fragile silk from her body. Just as their eyes made contact, his mouth came down to cover hers at the same time that his finger claimed her body.

Lucie arched wildly beneath his intimate touch, biting down on his bottom lip. He pulled back and explored the nick with his tongue, then kissed her again until she tasted blood. At the same time she felt his hand move between their bodies and guessed by his movements that he was undoing his pants. Confirmation came a second later when he removed his finger, replacing it with a shove from his massive cock.

"Aaaaggghhh!" she cried out in pleasure and some mild pain as his girth stretched her channel.

"Aaaaaaaaaaaggghhhh!" he groaned low between his teeth. "You're fucking tight!" Once he was all the way in he became still.

Lucie took the moment to let it all sink in, the feel of being stuffed, the feel of his hands gripping her hips. As their gazes remained locked, their breathing heavy, she squeezed her muscles around his shaft, watching with relish when he closed his eyes and sucked in his breath. Their heartbeats were one. Before long he started to move, slow at first, which nearly drove Lucie crazy. Every time he entered her body it tore a moan of pleasure from her.

She wished they'd taken the time to undress, but it didn't stop her from caressing him. Even through his clothes she could feel how hard his muscles were, feel them ripple beneath her hands. His thrusts were designed to give her the ultimate pleasure, hitting her sweet spot with mind-blowing accuracy. His speed picked up, and instinct guided her hands down his back to his taut buttocks. She clenched her hands into him. One more long glide against her clit and she was coming.

"Oh, God!" she cried, clenching tightly around his cock. She raised her head enough to bite his chin in passion. That was all it took and he rammed forward one last time, filling her cunt with streams of hot cum.

"Fuck!' he rasped, his body bucking uncontrollably against Lucie.

His hands gripped her hips almost painfully, holding her where he wanted her. Lucie was helpless beneath him, jerking with the convulsions of a powerful release intensified by his. Their breaths were ragged, and it seemed that a long time passed before their bodies calmed into a kind of blissful state. With the calm came the realization of several things for Lucie—they hadn't used protection and she didn't even know his name. Both a first for her, which revealed to her how distracting and powerful her lust for him had been.

"What's your name?" The words were spoken against the side of her neck.

"Lucie and yours?"

"Harry," he rasped.

A shiver rolled through Lucie when his cock slowly slipped out of her pussy. "I've never done anything like this before," she murmured quietly.

Harry raised his head. Their eyes met. "It's a first for me, too," he said. "I'm sorry if I was a little rough–"

"No, I–" Lucie felt her cheeks fill with heat.

"That's what you get when you tease the wrong man," he said softly.

"You looked like you handled it well."

He chuckled. "You left me with a hard-on and the name of your hotel."

"So you decided to come looking for me?"

"I figured you for a tourist and knew finding you wouldn't be hard. Most tourists don't spend much time in their hotel rooms."

"So, palace guards get days off?"

"The official title is the Queen's Guard." All at once he rolled, pulling Lucie with him. "How much time do we have before your friends return?"

"You take a lot for granted," Lucie commented, the teasing fingers against the back of her thighs tickling her. When they roamed over her naked butt she automatically squirmed away, thrusting her lower body against his.

His cock wasn't as soft as it had been.

He grunted. "I want more than one good fuck with you, lady." She felt his hands move up to the zipper at the top of her dress. "I want you naked, wet, and wild." He slowly began to lower the zipper down her back. "I'm leaving on a new assignment in two days and this is going to have to last me a long time."

Oh, God! Lucie was already wet. She wanted to ask Harry what assignment he was talking about but the only thing she could concentrate on was the sound of the zipper and the feel of his hand traveling down her backside. She caught her breath when he pushed her away from him, her dress falling away from her body and exposing her full breasts to him. His gaze caressed them with appreciation and growing hunger, scorching her where his eyes lingered.

"Very nice," he said, pulling Lucie's dress down to her waist, giving him easier access to the flesh he wanted. Then, lifting her upward, Harry settled her above him so that her breasts were dangling directly over his waiting mouth.

"Oh!" He put his warm mouth over the peaks, drawing on it while rolling the nipple with his tongue. Lucie felt instant wet heat gather between her legs. He took his time, suckling, tonguing, and nipping at both breasts and nipples, while his cock grew bigger and longer against her sex.

Finally pulling back, Harry looked into Lucie's eyes long and hard, as if he were trying to make up his mind about something. Before she could question him he reversed their positions until she was flat upon her back again. In record time he stripped her dress the rest of the way off, tossing it to the floor. His jacket and shirt followed, and as he worked at getting his pants and shoes off Lucie kicked off her heels.

Naked, aroused, and breathing heavily, they each took a moment to look one another over. Lucie marveled all over again at how muscular and battle-scarred Harry was. She reached forward and carefully traced a long jagged scar that ran halfway down his masculine chest. "It appears that the Queen's Guard is a dangerous job."

Harry watched her finger move on to another scar. "It can be, but I got most of these at the front lines in Afghanistan."

Because he was kneeling over her with his knees on the bed on either side of her she was able to sit up. Leaning forward, she kissed his chest, and then lightly ran the tip of her tongue down the scar she'd traced earlier. He sucked in his breath with a hiss, prompting Lucie to raise her gaze to his. Without warning he grabbed her by the arms and jerked her closer.

"I have a feeling it's going to be hard leaving you." Harry kissed her passionately, then, before Lucie could catch her breath, he raised his body slightly and flipped her onto her belly. Following her down, he nestled his cock between her legs.

The blood in Lucie's veins bubbled hotly, matching the fire pulsing in her pussy. Harry's cock throbbed strongly, adding further stimulation. She began to whimper and moan, silently pleading with him to fuck her again. She felt his warm breath against the side of her neck as he leaned in to kiss beneath her ear.

"You smell good," he whispered, nuzzling Lucie in the hair next to her ear. "The same scent that nearly drove me crazy the other day." His hands began to smooth over Lucie, touching all of her intimate places and discovering what pleased her. "You're a damned attractive woman." He tugged on her ear, and then traced the shell with his tongue. "Feel what you do to me?" She nodded, quivering. "Feel how hard you make my cock? What should I do about it?"

Lucie pushed her rear against his cock, moaning softly. "There's two holes down there, stick it in somewhere." She was so turned-on that she didn't know what she was saying, but she didn't care, even knowing that if he chose her anus it would hurt like hell. She could handle a little pain as long as she felt pleasure in the end.

Harry chuckled huskily. "Tempting." Suddenly his hands were on her ass, spreading the cheeks so he could tease her with the head of his cock. A whimper escaped her. There was no denying the lubricant he was spreading against the pucker of her anus was pre-cum. "So fucking tempting." She could tell by the change in his tone that he was losing control.

She braced herself for penetration, but she worried for nothing. Harry surprised her by lifting slightly, slipping an arm between Lucie's waist and the bed, and pulling her to her knees. She arched back, inviting him in, only he seemed content to rub the head of his cock up and down the seam of her pussy. Then ever so slowly he parted the plump lips and teased her clit a little before slipping past her labia and burying himself balls deep.

"Sweet Jesus, you have a tight cunt."

His words and the new position drove Lucie wild. Arching her butt as high as she could, she reached between them until she was able to fondle his balls.

"Holy shit!" He began to move as if the control had been taken away from him. With every slap of his testicles against the back of her thighs Lucie moved closer to orgasm. The air was thick with their combined arousal, and their mutual sounds of pleasure gave evidence to the intense ecstasy they were experiencing.

As Harry's movements became faster and rougher, Lucie sensed that he was getting close. One large hand grabbed a breast, while the other inched down her body to her clit. His finger circled the swollen nub then dipped into her pussy. *Oh, God!* He was so close to her G-spot! The thought alone almost made her come. Then, as if sensing her needs, he took his cock in his hand and with well-aimed thrusts managed to hit the sensitive area several times before getting them both off.

They cried out simultaneously, coming loud and hard. Harry held on to Lucie's hips, grinding his cock into her cunt as far as it would go. They convulsed together as they moved uncontrollably, draining the lust and passion until sweet exhaustion claimed them.

Chapter 4

"Do you have someone special in the states?"

Lucie shook her head. "Not for a while now." She almost hated to ask, surely a man as sexy as Harry had a girlfriend. "You?"

"No one."

Thank goodness for that. But what did it really matter? She lived in New York; he lived in England and was going on a mission soon. This encounter was the equivalent of a one-night-stand. "Where is your next assignment?" They were lying side by side, he on his stomach and she on her back. She glanced over at him.

He looked at her long and hard, his expression impossible to read. "I can't tell you, it's classified." He was serious, and the way his eyes narrowed on her, Lucie got the impression he was trying to determine her curiosity in asking.

"Oh. So you, ah, just guard the palace during your spare time?"

"Not exactly."

Why was he being so mysterious? She raised her upper body, resting on her elbows, watching his gaze drop lazily to her breasts. "You're full of secrets, aren't you?" Her comment drew his eyes back to hers and the silence grew. She wondered what he was thinking. "I know," she began in a teasing tone. "You're an undercover agent working for the Queen."

The slightest change came over his expression, revealing that her remark hit close to the truth. When a slight smile replaced the serious look on Harry's face she didn't let it fool her into thinking that he was going to confess anything. She had a feeling he could be very dangerous under the right circumstances.

"Let's just say that the services I perform are highly top secret. I go where I'm needed and do what I'm good at." He reached over and began to caress the breast closest to him. "Right now the only undercover position I'm interested in is fucking you."

Lucie caught her breath, his comment making her hot. She closed her eyes and purred. Harry's touch was sending shock waves of pleasure down to her pussy. "So, what are you good at?" She could hear the trembling emotion in her tone.

His chuckle was low and gruff. "I'm good at a lot of things. One of which is hunting down pretty American girls intent on driving us Brits insane with the promise of their sweet bodies." Lucie caught her breath when he gave her nipple a not-so-gentle pinch. "What do you do for a living?"

"I work in a legal office in New York City." She went willingly as Harry rolled onto his back, dragging her with him. "Have you ever been to the United States?"

"Several times, for business. Never for fun, but I'm thinking that might change in the near future." He began to caress her backside. "When do you go home?"

"In three more days," she said, wondering but hesitant to ask when he had to leave for his assignment.

"Good." He kissed her long and hard, firing up the passion between them again. By the time they parted they were both gasping for breath. "I want to fuck you again." His caresses became rougher, revealing how turned on he was.

"What's stopping you?" Lucie asked against his mouth. His response was to kiss her passionately. After a few moments of devouring each other's lips Harry tangled his fingers in the back of her hair and pulled her away. "Fuck me with your mouth," he rasped.

He didn't have to ask her twice. Lucie loved giving head. She kissed and bit her way down his powerful body, reveling in his wild response as she went along. Her hand locked onto his shaft, caressing the hard muscle up and down. Reaching where his cock jetted straight up from his loins, she sat back a moment to examine her prize.

She began to salivate. "Magnificent," she whispered in awe, meaning it, and finding it hard to believe he'd managed to stuff his impressive size inside her body. Seeing it up close, inhaling the musky scent of drying cum urged her to get down to business. It was obvious that Harry thought so too when his hand, still at the back of her head, forced her down. Lucie opened her mouth and slowly lowered it over his cock.

She moaned as her taste buds exploded with the texture and flavor of Harry's warm shaft. He groaned low, his hand holding Lucie from moving away while he thrust up and further into her mouth. When the knob of his cock was at the back of her throat she swallowed, causing him to groan again. Gradually the pressure of his hand was removed and Lucie was able to move on her own. She grazed her teeth carefully along the length of his rod, following it with the caress of her tongue.

"Fuck, you have a talented mouth." His thighs quivered as he thrust up and down into Lucie's mouth. Relishing in her power, she took a moment to lick his balls. "Aaaagghh!"

Smiling, Lucie swallowed his cock again, and began using her hand to pump the lower half close to his testicles. His speed picked up and she knew that he was getting ready to come. A few seconds later she felt the warm, salty thickness of cum coat her tongue and splash against the back of her throat.

"Aaaaggggggghhhh!" Harry groaned, letting go. "Aaaggghhh!" He convulsed as his orgasm exploded from him in waves.

Lucie milked his cock until it began to diminish. Once it slipped out of her mouth Harry reached for her and pulled her up his winded body. She fell halfway across his chest and he surprised her by kissing her.

"I want to see you again before I leave. Will you go to dinner with me tomorrow night?" Lucie nodded, secretly happy that he wasn't just going to walk out of her life as if nothing had happened between them. Her response seemed to please him. "And wear that little red number again. You looked damned hot in that." His hand was smoothing up and down her back.

She'd have to send it out to be cleaned. "Okay."

"I'd like us to exchange personal information so we can stay in touch." His comment surprised, yet pleased, Lucie.

Even though he'd given her an out, Lucie had a strong feeling that it wouldn't be that easy. The way he'd pursued her and taken control, Harry gave her the impression that he usually got what he wanted. Her thoughts flashed back to the day before when he'd been standing guard at Buckingham Palace. It was hard picturing him in that red uniform now, standing so straight and firm, when she knew him as a man of action.

"Unless you're not interested?"

She smiled. "I'd like that. This whole situation, what we did, is new for me. I think I'd feel a little bit sad if we just said goodbye and that was the end of it. It would be nice if we can remain... friends."

"Friends?" His laugh sounded a little bit gruff. "I think a trip to New York as a tourist is in order."

"In between your undercover work?" She couldn't help asking. Their gazes remained locked, and Lucie could tell that he was thinking things over. "Are you even in the British Army?"

The slightest smile curved his sexy bottom lip up at the corners. "I was a Grenadier Guard for ten years. Once a Grenadier, always a Grenadier."

Lucie was truly curious now. She'd read up enough to know Foot Guards came from five different regiments of the British Army, including the Grenadier Guard. Only he'd said it in the past tense. "Was?"

She felt his slight shrug. "I still serve the monarchy but in a different capacity."

"Undercover," she said, getting a slap on the behind for her insistence. "Ouch!"

Harry laughed. "Yes, 'undercover,' if using that term makes you happy."

"I knew it!" Lucie smiled in spite of the sting of his slap. "So what you were doing yesterday was undercover work?" He slapped her again. This time she only gasped.

"Enough, before I start to think you're a spy I should be interrogating."

"Well, you are slapping me," Lucie teased, reaching back to rub her behind.

"I'm beginning to like it," Harry admitted, thrusting his renewed hard-on against her. "You have a nice ass."

"Would you like to fuck it?" She knew that was an outrageous thing to say but couldn't help wanting to see how he'd react.

"Oh hell!" He shuddered. "You know just what to say to make me crazy," he growled, kissing Lucie roughly. During their heated kiss, which included a lot of tongue action, he turned, pulling her beneath him.

Lucie had never met such a man. He was about ten years older than she was; maybe it was their age difference. He was more experienced and manly compared to the guys she'd dated back home. His kisses and touches turned her blood hot and caused a sharp thrill to course through her aroused body. She began to tremble in response to his throbbing, hard cock, and the anticipation of having him inside her again. She touched him wherever she could, silently urging him to do whatever he wanted.

As Harry slipped his cock inside her waiting pussy Lucie knew that it was just the beginning of a long, special friendship, and possibly more.

The End

Party Time

Chapter 1

"Simon says, 'everyone remove your shirts.'"

I smiled at Devon's command, glad that I hadn't been suckered into the adult version of the game with the rest of them. They all knew Devon wouldn't pass up a chance to see some naked titties, and the rules were that once you agreed to play you couldn't drop out. I'd learned real quick which games were safe.

The women playing Simon Says giggled like school girls as they removed their blouses. It was clear by their fancy, naughty bras that they'd been expecting to show them off at some point during the party. It was no big deal for the men to remove their shirts, and they stood back with big, stupid grins on their faces, eyeing the ladies with obvious appreciation.

"Why aren't you playing?"

I turned to look at my older sister, Jenny. "I'm not stupid, and I know Devon. As soon as he joined I knew if he ever got to be Simon that our clothes would be coming off."

"Simon says, 'everyone jump up and down.'"

Jenny laughed and rolled her eyes. "He'll never change." I shook my head in silent agreement, sensing that she wanted to say something more. After a slight hesitation she asked, "RJ is back, did you see him?"

Why was her smile so sad? "Look, Jen, I've been over RJ for a long time. You don't have to look at me like that every time his name is mentioned or when there's a chance we'll run into each other." I was lying through my teeth. If Jenny sensed it she wisely kept it to herself.

"I know, but…" She released a sigh. "I know how much you love him."

I met Jenny's eyes. "Loved," I emphasized. "How much I loved him." I wondered how many times I'd have to use that word in the past tense before it came true. "And yes, I saw him when he came in." Alone, thank God.

RJ would have been hard to miss. He was six feet four inches of solid sexy muscle, and as hard and tough as the Marine that he was. Arriving in faded jeans and a pull-over shirt that made his green eyes pop, he was the hottest man there. His black hair was short, and his five o'clock shadow reminded me of how good it felt against my inner thighs when he was using his tongue on my pussy.

I squeezed my eyes shut and willed the erotic image away, but it was no use. When we'd been together we'd had an over-active sex life, never wasting an opportunity to hide away somewhere and fuck each other until we were exhausted. There were times when I'd thought we were going to consume one another, when we couldn't seem to get enough, especially when RJ came home after a long stint away in the Marines. His hunger had fed mine.

How long had he been gone this time? About eight months. I glanced around. The party was in full swing, and wherever I looked there were people standing around in groups, talking and laughing while they drank, some reaching for a snack off of one of the many trays being paraded around the room. I tried not to be obvious as I searched for RJ. He'd come alone but with his rugged, dark looks I knew that he wouldn't remain that way for long.

Well, speak of the devil, I thought, looking toward the opened French doors that led to the dance area outside. RJ sauntered in, looking confident and like a man who didn't have a care in the world. It made me angry that he might have gotten over me a lot sooner than

I'd gotten over him. I'd thought about him the whole time he was gone, and had missed the hell out of him. When a woman joined him a few seconds later I saw red, curling my nails into my palms.

It was Layla, someone I'd gone to school with but had never really been a friend of mine. Living in a small town, everyone knew everyone and it wasn't uncommon for people to show up at an event together. Barely decent in a red dress, Layla linked her arm through RJ's and rubbed her well endowed breasts against him. I wanted to go over there, rip her away from him, and snatch out all of her bottle blonde hair.

All of a sudden RJ was looking my way. I don't know why I did it but I panicked and grabbed the closest man to me. I couldn't bear for RJ to see me standing there alone. I barely had time to register that I'd grabbed RJ's best friend, Ray, before planting my lips firmly on his. He resisted for only a second before I felt him relax and kiss me back.

I had only intended to kiss Ray long enough to make certain that RJ saw us, but when I went to draw back his arms locked my body against his and he forced my mouth to open against his. I moaned in protest as he used his tongue as a battering ram against mine, taking what I was unwilling to give. *How dare he!* Finally, after a few seconds more, he pulled away and winked.

"What the hell, Ray–"

"Is he looking?" he asked, undaunted by my anger.

"What?"

"RJ, is he looking?"

I peeked in the direction I'd seen RJ. "Yes!" I was still simmering.

"Good. Then our little show wasn't wasted." Ray looked very pleased with himself. "Maybe this will speed things up. You and RJ belong together."

"I didn't kiss you to make him jealous."

"Didn't you?"

"No, I didn't. I didn't want him to—" I stopped what I'd been about to say. It made me sound so pathetic.

"See you all alone?" Ray finished for me. I reluctantly nodded. "Well, now he thinks you're with me. Use it any way you want."

Ray walked away, and I wondered what he'd meant by his last comment. I glanced at the French doors, finding that RJ was gone. Apparently the kiss Ray and I had shared hadn't made him jealous enough to hang around and see what else we might share. Disappointment raced through me. Oh, God, had I made things worse?

RJ had a jealous streak a mile long, and his lack of reaction told me that he didn't care.

Chapter 2

RJ *Fuck!* What I wouldn't give for a cigarette. The only time I really missed them was after fucking Georgia, and I'd given them up for her. Now, after seeing her with Ray's tongue halfway down her throat I needed something to take the edge off. If I hadn't walked away when I did, Ray would be on his way to the hospital and I'd be on my way to jail. *Fuck! Fuck! Fuck!* How had I not known that they were together? Ray hadn't said anything the last time we talked.

As one of the waitresses walked by with a tray, I grabbed a glass of scotch, downed it in one swallow, and replaced it with another. I made my way to the far corner of the backyard where it was dark and quiet. I found a bench and sat down, sighing deeply. For eight fucking months I'd thought about Georgia, dreamt about her, masturbated with her on my mind, and I'd come home to this shit? I shook my head, growing angrier by the second.

I reminded myself that I was the reason that we'd broken up, but deep down I guess I'd always thought that we'd get back together. We always had before. But it was obvious she'd moved on this time, and with my best friend. How was I supposed to handle that? I loved Ray like a brother, but how was I supposed to go through the rest of my life knowing he had the woman I wanted? Knowing that he was kissing and touching her, *fucking* her. Had they already fucked? Oh, hell I didn't want to think about that. The thought of him sliding his cock inside Georgia made my blood pressure rise. The little sounds of pleasure she made at that precise moment would forever be etched in my subconscious.

I downed my second glass of scotch and tossed the glass into the bushes. From my position I could see inside the open French doors. I was surprised to see Georgia emerge outside with another man and walk out onto the dance floor with him. Instant jealousy took control of my common sense when she let him pull her against his body as they began to dance. Where the hell was Ray? When Georgia was mine no other man had touched her, or held her. Before I realized what I was doing I was fisting my hands.

I took a deep breath and got to my feet. If Ray wasn't going to look out for his woman then I would do it for him. That's what friends did—they had each other's backs. As I walked towards Georgia I let my eyes roam over her, and not for the first time that evening. She was wearing a dress. Something soft and flowery that left her shoulders bare, along with most of her pretty legs. I couldn't help but notice how nicely the top shaped her full breasts, showing just enough cleavage to draw a man's gaze there, my gaze.

She'd pulled her long strawberry blonde hair up with a clip, only some curls had escaped to lie against the back of her neck. The closer I got, the more I was able to take in her perfume, the perfume I'd bought her for her last birthday. It's light, fresh scent sucked me in and suddenly I wanted to taste her. I breathed in deeply for control, and tapped the man's shoulder.

"Excuse me." I knew my unfriendly tone didn't leave anything open for interpretation. The guy didn't hesitate in turning Georgia loose and stepping aside. Before she could recover from my taking over I took her into my arms. "Ray doesn't mind you dancing with other men?" I tried to ignore the instant awareness that having her against me pulled from my body. "When you were my woman–"

"But I'm not your woman anymore," Georgia said, cutting me off. "You gave up any rights you had over me before you left for deployment the last time. I'm free to be with whoever I want."

Yes, I'd thought I was doing her a favor. I didn't think it was fair for her to have to always be waiting for me to come home, *if* I came home. Once I'd decided to make the Marines my career I'd known that there would always be a goodbye between us. I should have reminded myself how damned good it felt coming home to her and having her in my arms again.

"So you and Ray aren't a couple?"

She hesitated as if she were considering her answer before saying, "Not exclusively."

Not exclusively? "I saw the kiss you planted on him earlier."

She shrugged. "Maybe we just like kissing."

Her carefree remark made me angry. "What else do you like doing together?"

"What do you think, RJ? Ray's your best friend, you should know."

Yeah, I knew. It wouldn't be the first time one of my ex-girlfriends had moved on to Ray. Ray liked his women quiet and petite, and he preferred red heads, not leggy blondes who weren't afraid to say what was on their minds. Georgia was all that, and more. She was passionate in and out of the bed. The fact they weren't exclusive sent up a red flag, but also told me that I wouldn't be infringing if I were to make any moves on Georgia.

And there was one specific move I wanted to make.

I was growing hard against her, which was nothing new. She'd always had that affect over me, more than any other woman. As I looked down into her face, taking note of the natural color in her smooth cheeks and the fullness of her sexy bottom lip, I decided to give in to a need I'd never been able to control around her. I didn't give her time to do anything other than accept my hard kiss.

Oh, sweet Jesus she tasted good. There were strawberries on her breath, and I got a better taste when I pushed my tongue into her warm, wet mouth. Her sweet moan of acceptance, and the way she melded against me turned my cock to stone-hard fucking mode. Georgia knew her little moans of pleasure got to me; she knew what it did to me to know that she was aroused. As our tongues explored, tasted, and battled vigorously, I lowered my hands to her sweet ass and pulled her sharply against my dick.

The music stopped, but we didn't. I was vaguely aware that someone was announcing that it was time for strip poker and everyone was leaving to go inside. I was glad to see Christa's parties were as wild as ever and her adult version of strip poker had always been the highlight, drawing in almost everyone who was there. It left the backyard to me and Georgia and the plans that I had for her. I pulled back and looked into her dazed eyes.

"That didn't even begin to take the edge off," I admitted in a raspy voice that sounded like a different man.

"Edge?" Georgia asked in a breathy whisper.

"Of seeing you and Ray kissing." I squeezed her luscious ass to punish her, enjoying her whimper. "Since you and Ray aren't exclusive, then he won't mind if I fuck you."

She gasped.

"And I intend to fuck the hell out of you."

Chapter 3

Georgia

Ohmygod! I knew my panties were wet. Kissing RJ after all these months apart had put my body into instant arousal. Having his hands on me added fuel, and feeling his large cock throb against me almost sent me over the edge. Maybe he was reacting to my kissing Ray, but he'd always been possessive where I was concerned and his actions now proved that he was still into me. All his crap about me moving on and meeting someone to have a normal life with went up in smoke if this was his reaction to just seeing me kissing another man. *Thank you, Ray.*

Inside I was elated. RJ had to know that I still loved him. I don't think anything would ever change that. As always my body flooded with a pleasant warmth of need and acceptance when RJ admitted his hunger for me. First his body, then his mouth, and I was lost. His cock was pushing insistently against my lower belly now, and all I could think about was how fast I could get it inside me and how incredibly awesome it would feel. Suddenly he was taking my hand and pulling me along.

"Where are we going?" It was hard to keep up with him in heels.

"I know of a dark, quiet spot where we won't be interrupted." He was taking a lot for granted, assuming that I was his for the taking. "If I don't get inside your cunt soon I'm going to explode."

"But we're broken-up," I reminded him teasingly, a little breathless from our fast pace. I wasn't going to make it easy for him after the eight months of grief that he'd put me through. His gruff laugh ran over me, leaving me tingling in places that begged for his hands. "You told me to move on, to find someone else."

He halted and turned my way. "Did you?"

"You saw me kissing Ray."

He jerked me to him roughly and gritted, "Damnit, Georgia, I'm not in the mood for games. Did you move on?"

I felt tears of emotion fill my eyes. *Why couldn't he love me the way that I loved him?* "Never," I croaked.

Groaning, RJ kissed me passionately for several long seconds. When it was over he picked me up and I wrapped my legs around his waist. Several steps later he was lowering us onto a bench.

"God, baby, don't cry," he said between kisses as his lips moved over my face. "I didn't mean to hurt you." He kissed his way down my throat. "For eight months you've been haunting me, day and night," he murmured, working his way over my bare shoulders. "I'm a stupid, stupid man."

His comment brought a smile to my mouth. "We agree on something," I said softly, leaning my head back so that he had easier access to my neck. "Fuck me, RJ," I pleaded, running my hands up his back and beneath his shirt. "I need you."

A deep growl escaped him and then he was undoing the buttons that lined the bodice of my dress. Next he slipped it all the way down, exposing my full breasts to the moonlight. He wasted no time in lifting and loving them with his hands and mouth, causing little ripples of ecstasy to wash over me. I eagerly arched my back and thrust out my breasts as he suckled and nipped at my hard nipples. Then, just as rapidly, his hand snaked beneath my skirt and inched its way up my thigh.

He didn't waste any time, tugging away the fragile silk that covered my mound and tossing it to the ground, ruined. I crushed my face into his shoulder and let out a muffled cry when his finger entered my body. "Oh, God, RJ!" I panted, shivering wildly against him. "I–" I just barely caught myself from telling him that I loved him. Instead, I concentrated on the pleasure that his finger was giving as he moved it in and out, slowly, teasing my G-spot and clit with the unspoken promise of ecstasy.

After having gone eight months without his particular brand of making love, it didn't take him long to get me there. My orgasm raced to the finish line, exploding onto his finger and beyond. As I could do nothing but ride the wave to completion, I convulsed helplessly against RJ, clenching my hands into the muscles of his arms. "I need you inside me," I whispered against his throat. I bit him in the way that I knew he liked.

Wordlessly we worked together to free his cock. As soon as the massive muscle was out RJ lifted me and lowered me onto it. Inch-by-slow-inch he filled my still-pulsing cunt until he was so far in that my ass was on his balls. Mutual sounds of carnal bliss floated away into the darkness, drowned out by the sounds of music and laughter that were coming from inside the house.

"You have a tight cunt, baby," RJ said in a low tone. He put his hands on my hips and began to lift me up and down. "Damn, I've missed you." He kissed me tenderly, but the longer his mouth moved over mine and our tongues meshed together, the hungrier I became.

I began to move with him, twitching every time he brushed against my sweet spot. Before long I had moved my hand between us so that I could play with my clit. I felt him smile against my lips as his hand nudged mine away so he could take control.

He ended our kiss. "Next time I want to suck your clit," he said, circling it with his finger. "I want your cum on my tongue."

Next time? "Oh, fuck!" His words made me hotter, and he knew it. I began to ride his cock like it was a bucking bronco.

"Easy, baby."

"It's... your... fault," I said between pants. "You... know dirty... talk gets to... me every time." Two could play at that game. "I want your... cum in my... cunt," I said, grinding my butt against him. "No condom this time, RJ, I mean it."

"Oh, shit!" RJ exclaimed, shuddering. He leaned back on the bench and thrust his loins upward. Now his cock was going in as far as it could, until it hit against something. I clenched my muscles as hard as I could, getting a deep grunt for my efforts. He was fucking me so fast that I had to clutch his shoulders to remain in place.

"Oh, yeah, baby," I closed my eyes and enjoyed the ride. "Fuck me harder. Fuck me faster." RJ grunted, his hands squeezing my breasts. I sensed the end was near. "I need to feel you come, RJ," I felt my own orgasm peak. "Come now!" I cried out, losing control.

We climaxed the same time. I knew it because RJ always finished in the same way. He fisted my hair close to my scalp, and kissed me roughly, letting go, convulsing against my body as his cock spewed ribbons of warm cum inside my body.

"Aaaaggghhh!" He groaned against my lips. "Oh, fuck, baby!" He kept me close as our convulsions slowed and gradually our body's calmed.

Chapter 4

Georgia

"We'd better get back to the party before someone comes looking for us." I was still sitting on RJ's lap, buttoning up the buttons over my breasts. "Like my sister." His cock was slowly deflating inside my body.

"Most everyone here knows about us," RJ said.

"Yes and what they know is that we broke up eight months ago." I couldn't stop the small sound of acknowledgement when his cock slipped out.

He chuckled. "There isn't one person in there who doesn't know what we're doing when we disappear."

He was right. The perils of living in a small town, and everyone knew that he'd just returned home from deployment. We'd been on-again, off-again for the last three years, and even though we'd just had sex, I wondered what our status was now. RJ had made it clear before he'd left the last time that it was over.

When he reached down to take care of himself and zip up his jeans, I scooted back closer to his knees so that he had easier access. I glanced down and watched him carefully tuck his cock behind his zipper area. As he was zipping up he glanced up and caught my smile. He smiled back.

"Stop looking at me that way or you're going to find yourself right back where you were five minutes ago."

"Eight months is a long time."

"I told you to move on."

I froze. His comment angered me. "So you would be okay if I'd fucked someone else while you were away?" His mouth tightened and I knew what the answer was without him voicing it. "You can't just break it off and tell me to move on, RJ. You may be able to turn off your feelings like a light switch but it's not that easy for me. I hate that you think all we have between us is sex."

Damnit, I felt my eyes tearing up again. I tried to get off his lap but his hands wrapped around my upper arms and held me firmly. I put my hands against his hard chest to keep him away. "You can't have it both ways, RJ. It's all or nothing, so make up your damn mind. You want me when it's convenient for you, well, I'm done letting you hurt me." I meant what I said, even though the thought of not having him in my life was tearing a hole in my heart. "I hope you enjoyed the fuck because it's the last one you'll be getting from me!"

For the first time since I'd known RJ he seemed speechless. He actually let me go this time, and I slid off his lap and walked away. Right before I stepped back inside the house I wiped my eyes and took a deep breath. Thank God the lights were dimmed and the place was packed. I made a quick sweep of the gyrating bodies, looking for Jenny, making my way to the bathroom. There was a line and I didn't feel like waiting. Knowing the layout of Christa's house, I headed for the stairs that would take me to the second floor.

I wasn't wearing underpants and I needed to clean up.

RJ

I watched Georgia walk away, damning myself for being a fool. She was the best thing that had ever happened to me and I couldn't say the words she needed to hear. My career choice didn't leave much left over for a wife and family. Oh, I knew a lot of Marines had families, and over the years I'd witnessed a lot of depressing goodbyes. The weeping and miserable looks on tear streaked faces and the kids clinging to their father's legs and begging them not to go had been enough for me to make a hard decision. I didn't want to put someone I loved through that.

I loved Georgia with everything in me. She was wrong, the sex was fucking fantastic, but it wasn't the only thing we had. As she disappeared through the open French doors I got to my feet and headed that way. I needed another drink, and I wanted to find Georgia to make sure she was okay.

"Hey, man." Ray saw me as soon as I walked into the house. "Looks like you can use this more than me." He handed me his drink. I just glared at him. "Don't give me that look. Someone had to show you how you'd feel seeing another man kissing her."

"Not my best friend," I said.

"Why not? You'd rather see her in the arms of someone else? At least with me you know it wasn't serious."

I downed his drink and handed him back his glass. "Like hell. You had your tongue halfway down her throat. You're lucky I don't stomp the crap out of you." Then something Ray said registered with me. "So you two aren't together?"

"Hell no, man. You know I don't have it in me to be faithful to one woman. But I'm telling you, RJ, if you don't make things right with Georgia, you're a damned fool. She's the best thing you've got going, and she turned down a lot of dates while you were gone."

I frowned. "How do you know that?"

He shrugged. "Small town, word gets around." Something caught his eye and I followed the direction Ray was looking to see the object of our discussion walking down the stairs. "Look at her, RJ." I did. "Now look around you."

It didn't take me long to figure out what Ray meant. More than one man had his gaze on Georgia, following her with appreciation and lust in their eyes. It made me want to fight, and I realized that if I wasn't careful the feeling would take control of my actions. I blamed it on my training as a Marine because I always felt battle-ready.

Georgia was oblivious to the stares. As she neared the bottom of the steps a smile spread across her face, and I watched as she took Mike Danvers' hand and was pulled into a tight group of dancers. I glanced back at Ray. He raised his brows but didn't say anything. He didn't need to. I knew that 'what are you gonna do about it' look. I clenched my teeth and searched the gyrating bodies for Georgia, catching a glimpse of her before she disappeared again.

"Hey, everyone!"

RJ turned in the direction that the loud voice was coming from to see Christa standing on top of a table. The background noise had almost drowned her out. She motioned to someone and suddenly the music stopped, and so did everyone else.

"Let's get this party hopping!" she shouted enthusiastically, receiving cheers and encouragement in return. Christa had a reputation for throwing wild parties and I couldn't help but wonder what she had planned.

"Time for another round of sexy games! The only rule is if you stay you play! No one standing off to the side just watching." Laughter sounded through the room. "The earlier games of strip poker, naked Twister, and spin the bottle should have warmed you up. Now it's time for Russian roulette, dares in a hat, and suck and blow! The ones out on the patio, the twos in the living room, and the threes over by the dining room."

"Did you pick a number when you came in?" Ray asked me.

I shook my head no and he walked away. I wasn't one for playing games, even adult games. I watched as everyone seemed to scramble to their respective areas. My interest was on Georgia. As soon as I found her I narrowed my gaze and kept it trained on her, like a predator zeroing in on its prey. In a way that's what I was, because I hungered for her, and I knew before the night was over that I was going to consume her.

I'd tasted her passion once that evening, and once wasn't enough.

Chapter 5

Georgia

I walked out onto the patio with the rest of the ones, surprised to see Jenny and Ray in the group. My sister settled next to me as we formed a large circle. In the center there was a small table with a top hat on it, and inside the hat were scraps of paper. Each paper held a to-do on it that had to be performed by the person who picked it. It could be an individual act, or something they had to do with someone else. If that person decided not to do the act, they had to swallow a shot of vodka and pick another paper. They were not allowed to have two drinks in a row. A table had been set up to the side with shots already prepared.

I pretended not to notice RJ as he watched from the shadows. It was obvious that he didn't intend to play, until Christa walked through the door and gave him no choice. She pushed him toward us.

"Come on, RJ, You know the rules."

He didn't protest as he took a spot next to Ray. His eyes were fixed on me in a way that I knew only too well. I felt my nipples harden and cursed my weakness. *Damn him!* Why did I have to love him? I thought about leaving, but refused to let him see what he was doing to me. His interest dropped slowly down my body, drawing out a response I couldn't hope to control. When his gaze returned to mine, and I saw the humor dancing in his, I let my gaze roam over him just as slowly and thoroughly. There was no denying the lust reflected in his dark eyes when our gazes locked the next time.

Christa's cheerful voice interrupted the moment. "Okay, it was determined early on that Jenny will go first. So come on up and pick a piece of paper from the hat."

Tossing me a smile, my sister fairly danced her way to the top hat. She made a show of looking everywhere but at what she was doing, as she reached inside and drew out a small piece of paper. "Oh, boy," she laughed, before reading what the note said. "Kiss the first woman to my right."

A chorus of laughter broke out because I was the first woman to her right. I'm sure whoever wrote the note was expecting something a lot racier than the quick peck on the cheek Jenny gave me.

Once Christa seemed satisfied with how the dares in a hat game was going she took off. The next person to go was on the other side of Jenny, which meant that I would be last. I didn't mind. Most of the commands were outrageous, like remove your clothes down to your underwear, lick the belly of someone of the same sex, hump the leg of the person standing directly across from you, suck on someone's fingers, and so on. The vodka disappeared fast but some of the group had no problem carrying out what their paper said.

Then it was RJ's turn to draw. He reached in, drew out a paper, opened it, and looked directly at me. "Pass this request on to someone else."

"What's the request?" A few people asked, only RJ remained quiet.

He walked directly to me and handed me the note. I glanced down at it and groaned.

"What's it say?" Their tones revealed their impatience.

"It says to make-out with the person who gave me the note." I didn't appreciate the laughter that followed, or the amused gleam in RJ's eyes or Rays either, for that matter. I was determined to have the last laugh. "I think I'll pass on this and take a drink." My decision didn't have the desired effect and only made that sexy-as-sin-smile widen more on RJ's mouth.

I put the note in the trash basket beneath the table and went to the liquor table for my first shot. I didn't hesitate, but maybe I should have. I swallowed the vodka in one swallow and it took my breath away. I knew better than to do that, but the teasing comments over my preferring the drink over kissing RJ made me reckless.

"You have to draw another note from the hat," someone said. "Then we go back to the person we left off at."

I grabbed the first paper my fingers fell on, opened it up, and read it. *What?* I read it again with disbelief. Of all the luck! I took a deep breath. "Turn someone on without touching them."

"Oh, that's a good one!" someone laughed.

"You have to do it, too. You can't have another drink. That's the rule."

I turned and glared at Jenny. She just looked back at me with an innocent look on her face, and then I glanced around the circle of friends. I'd known most of them for years, had gone to school with and grown up with them. But there was no one there that I cared to turn on, with the exception of RJ. Then I set my eyes on Ray, and for just a minute I pondered picking him. The look on his face was priceless, almost panicked, but it was RJ's expression that gave me pause.

We stood there, staring into each other's eyes. I could feel my heart beating and my breathing becoming shallow. I didn't have to wonder about the passion in his eyes or the raw desire etched on his sharp features. I was sure that it mirrored mine. I thought about our earlier love-making and closed my eyes. Big mistake! My body responded to that hot memory and suddenly I wanted to be back on that bench, riding his cock again. The trickle of wetness between my thighs reminded me that I didn't have any underwear on.

"Come on, Georgia, who do you pick?" Jenny asked.

Before I knew it, RJ had broken from the circle and was walking toward me. "No one," he said gruffly. "This party is over." He took my hand and pulled me away. I didn't look back. I didn't care if everyone knew what we would be doing when we finally ended up wherever it was he was taking me. I didn't care if it wasn't any further than that bench at the back of the yard, where everyone could hear me cry out my release. Unless I was mistaken, RJ had finally made a decision about us. I knew he wanted to fuck me, but I also sensed something different about him.

"Where are we going?" I had to practically run to keep up with him.

"Home," he said simply.

"My home or yours?"

"Mine." We cut across the neighbor's yard and headed for the street. "And unless you want me to stop right here and fuck you in the street I'd step up my pace."

A soft laugh escaped me in spite of his gruff threat. "Are you that horny? I didn't even get a chance to turn you on," I teased, thinking about the game." We reached the street, where his motorcycle was parked. Both sides of the street were packed with vehicles, thanks to Christa's party.

Without warning RJ stopped and pushed me up against the nearest car. I raised my face for his kiss, and wasn't disappointed when he swooped down and covered my mouth with his. The needy roughness of it made me hot, and I wrapped my arms around his neck to get closer to him. Groaning, he arched his hard cock into my lower body while his hands smoothed around to my butt. I could feel him pulling my dress up the back of my thighs, and we both lost control when his fingers squeezed into my naked buttocks.

"Holy shit!" he said against my mouth. "I forgot you aren't wearing anything under this dress." His open mouth ran up and down the side of my neck. "I don't know why I ever thought I could give you up. I love you, baby."

"I love you, too, RJ." I said breathlessly, trembling with hunger. "How about do us both a favor and get us home."

RJ

I gunned my motorcycle as fast as I dared, thankful that I didn't live far from Christa's. The vibration of the bike beneath me and Georgia's caresses kept me hard as stone. Her small hands moved underneath my shirt, gliding over my chest, abs, and lower belly as she held on behind me. As soon as I turned into my drive and turned the engine off I grabbed my helmet off her head and tossed it onto the grass. Then, I took her hand as we practically ran to the front door.

Once there I had to unlock it, but it took a while as Georgia's sweet kisses were very distracting. I barely took time to close and lock the door behind us once we were inside. By the time we reached my bedroom we were naked, leaving a trail of clothes behind. I pulled her around to face me, feasting my eyes on her naked beauty. Eight long months, and my dreams hadn't done her justice. She was a goddess with curves and I couldn't take my eyes off her rosy-tipped breasts and beautiful cunt. I reached up and pulled the clip from her hair, watching the long, soft mane fall all around her.

I released a groan of desire and tangled my fingers into her hair, jerking her against me and kissing her. Her hands touched my sides, before one traveled down to my aching cock. I didn't need to tell Georgia what to do or what I wanted. We knew each other, what gave each other pleasure, what bordered on pain, without having to voice it. It seemed that every time we fucked we discovered something new and pleasurable.

"God, baby, that feels good," I said against the softness of her mouth. Our tongues touch and explored the texture and flavor of each other's mouths. I moved my hips instinctively, pumping my cock into her hand, and nearly fell to my knees when she dropped to hers and took my shaft into her mouth.

I stared down at her. It always did something to me, seeing her like that, on her knees, her mouth swallowing my cock. I knew it wouldn't take me long to reach an orgasm, I could already feel it racing through me like hot lava. When my balls tightened against my body I pulled away and drew Georgia to her feet. In the next instant she was beneath me on the bed and I was fucking the hell out of her.

"RJ!" she cried out, her hands moving over me wherever she could reach. Her rapid breathing and the way she was arching into me told me that she was close to coming, too. As her cunt squeezed my dick I lost control, thrusting into her one last time and letting go.

The convulsions of her body told me she was climaxing. We held each other, riding out the wave together. I kissed her tenderly as our bodies calmed and our breathing slowed.

"Marry me before I go back oversees." I said, knowing that I wanted Georgia for my wife more than anything else. "I need you like I need air to breathe. Marry me, baby." I kissed her again, before pulling back and meeting the tears in her eyes. I could tell she was overcome with emotion and unable to speak. She nodded, her lips quivering.

My heart swelled. I'd almost thrown away the woman that I loved. I wouldn't make that mistake again.

The End

Lovers

Chapter 1

Angel stood back and surveyed her handiwork of the last few days. She pulled her gardening gloves off, casting a critical eye over the flower boxes beneath the windows of her older home, and the abundance of colorful wild flowers zooming up and over the edges. Wild flowers were her favorite because she could plant them anywhere and they would flourish and spread, and that's exactly what she wanted. They were beautiful against the backdrop of her freshly painted little white house.

There was plenty of lavender, her favorite, with daisies, false miterwort, marigolds, buttercups, daylilies, wood violets, and Queen Anne's lace mixed in. Angel had also spent hours planting them all along the sides of her house and detached garage, until from a distance her home resembled some of the country homes she'd seen in one of her favorite country magazines. Satisfied, she took a deep, fulfilling breath, and smiled.

"Looks good!"

She turned toward the road and returned Diana's wave as she sped past, heading toward town. *It does look good.* Angel was proud of all she'd accomplished since the tenting of her house for termites. Once she'd finished the light remodeling and painting of the inside she'd decided to tackle the outside. After forfeiting her usual vacation in the mountains in North Carolina at the last minute in order to spend time on her house, she was done.

Angel's gaze returned to the road. She could just make out the back end of Diana's car before it disappeared around the first bend. Another sigh, this time wistful, escaped her. These days she couldn't see or talk to Diana without thinking about her sexy brother, Bishop. The man Angel loved with all her heart.

Where is he, is he okay? She'd probably never get the answer to the first half of her thought because everything he did was top secret, and besides, he didn't like to talk about it. The answer to the second half of her concerns would come when she saw him again. After the night that he'd shown up at her home and they'd had smoking hot sex in her kitchen, they'd had two short days together before he'd been called back to duty. Angel remembered how hard it had been saying goodbye to him, just managing to hold back the tears until he drove away.

She'd been determined not to leave him with the memory of a clinging, weeping woman, something he'd confessed was one of the reasons he'd never settled down. But the second he was out of sight Angel had broken down, getting comfort from Diana, who'd been intuitive enough to show up right after her brother had left.

Thank God for Diana. They were more than co-workers and best friends, they were soul-sisters. Now that she and Bishop were involved, Diana had vocalized that they would also be sisters-in-laws one day. Angel had remained silent, yet hopeful. She knew Bishop felt something for her, but until he either figured out what it was or accepted it, she wouldn't get her hopes up. He'd been nothing but honest with her about his life choices and what he wanted for the future, but cautious enough in saying that they would take it one day at a time.

Angel didn't need any time. She'd marry the Navy SEAL tomorrow if he showed up and asked her. He'd been gone a little over a month but it seemed like forever to her. Though they were able to have a few stolen moments on Skype, and they were able to exchange emails, she missed his passionate kisses, his rough possession of her, and most of all she missed *him*. His company.

Crap. Realizing she was still standing at the end of her drive and staring at her house, she shook her head to clear it, but it didn't stop the tears from gathering in her eyes. As she began to slowly make her way back toward the house she heard a vehicle turn into her drive, the gravel crunching beneath the tires, and swung around. *Diana?* Lord, how long had she been standing there?

With a smile she walked back to where Diana had stopped her car. "Didn't you just drive past here to town?"

Diana laughed. "I just went down to the vegetable stand. Mrs. Crawley brings in her home- made breads and whoopee pies on Wednesdays. Here," she handed one to Angel, "I picked up a loaf of strawberry banana nut for you."

"Thanks," Angel said as she took it from her.

"Got a couple loaves for us, too. You know you can freeze it if you aren't in the mood for it right now."

"I might freeze half of it." Angel loved Mrs. Crawley's breads and pies, and often froze a few of them so she could have them during the winter months. Her stand was only open five months out of the year.

"The place looks terrific, Angel."

"I think so, too. The painters just finished up a few days ago."

"I thought they weren't going to paint the garage."

Angel smiled. "I plied them with daily lunches and drinks so they surprised me and added it in for free."

"That was nice of them! I love the wildflowers, too. Are you going to do anything to the back?"

Angel looked toward the rear of her property, which backed up to the woods. She thought about having a small garden this year but it was really too late now, she'd have to wait until spring, when the snow was gone and the ground was warmer. She shook her head. "Too late to have the garden I'd planned."

"Yeah, before long school will be in and it will be fall. Looking forward to seeing the kids again." They both taught classes at Ladybug Academy.

Angel nodded her agreement, asking, "Have you heard anything from Bishop?"

"No, honey. He won't be able to keep in touch when they're out in the field."

"I know. I just thought I'd ask." Angel tried to hide her disappointment.

"If he does get in touch it will most likely be with you, anyway," Diana said. "Look, why don't you come over for dinner this Saturday and plan to spend the night. Alex is going down to the coast Friday night and won't be back until Sunday. You know I don't like staying alone."

Angel knew that was true. Diana often asked her over when Alex was gone overnight. Come to think of it, she could use the company, too. Now that the house and yard was done she had nothing to do before going back to work, and these days she welcomed any distractions that took her mind off Bishop.

"What time?" Angel smiled.

"Whenever you're ready," Diana shrugged. "I'll make a big pitcher of margaritas and we'll have dirty rice and tacos for dinner." She put the car in reverse. "See you tomorrow!"

Angel watched her back out of the drive before turning to head inside.

Chapter 2

Fuck! Bishop lowered his head as pandemonium erupted all around them. Herc was laying half-in, half-out of a gutter, covered in mud and sewage in an effort to blend in. Wizard was ahead of them somewhere, rigging trip wires to slow down anyone coming after them, while Sniper was poised with his assault rifle in a tree to his right. Razor and Dogman had gone ahead with the package they were sent in to extract. All they had to do now was give Razor and Dogman enough of a head start so that they reached the rendezvous site before the helicopter took off.

Their orders had been explicit, and their window of opportunity was short. They had until thirteen hundred to make it back, or the pilot would take off, leaving them to make it back to base camp on foot. Not usually a problem for them, unless they had a package. More often than not any packages they extracted were civilians that slowed them down and created other problems. Bishop was pretty certain the sixty-five-year-old Ambassador would be a hindrance and that would put them all in extreme danger.

The lack of gunfire was a good sign, telling Bishop the kidnappers didn't realize which way they'd gone, and that they hadn't been spotted yet. Until then he and the rest of his team would remain stationary. It was times like now when he found it the hardest to keep Angel out of his head, and all he could think of was her sweet smile and passionate submission. All it took was closing his eyes and he could picture her alluring curves and the sparkle of desire in her pretty eyes.

Has it only been a week?

God, what he wouldn't give to have her under him now, naked and twisting, instead of the hard, wet ground. *Zing!* A shot rang out, and then more, cutting short his thoughts of Angel. He was on full alert again, twisting left, and then right to make sure the rest of his team were still situated where he'd last seen them. They would hold off as long as they could, and then reveal their positions by firing back.

Outnumbered three to one, they would kill as many as they could before retreating in time to meet the helicopter.

Zing! Zing! Zing!

As bullets hit the ground around them, Bishop realized that they needed to move. The terrorist cell, soldiers dressed in green combat fatigues, was running toward them and shooting wildly. Sniper was already taking careful aim and firing at the closest men, who were quickly replaced by others. Explosives detonated, and flying bodies indicated more casualties.

Zing! Zing!

Fuck it! If they didn't move soon they were dead men. He was about to make a move when Wizard burst onto the scene. That was their signal that it was time to go. The briefing prior to the mission had them forming a firing line as they began to retreat, stepping backwards to keep the opposition in sight.

Zing! Zing! Zing! Zing! Zing! Zing!

Enemy fire seemed to be coming from all directions. "Grenades!" Bishop yelled. With the exception of Sniper, who continued shooting, he, Wizard and Herc reached for the belts around their waists and pulled one from a pouch. Throwing them at the cluster of advancing men took out about half of them, the rest scattering as the firing continued.

Zing! Zing!

Bishop felt first one, and then a second bullet rip into him. *Holy shit, that hurts!* He stumbled to his knees, and then tried to get to his feet, only to fall again. *Fuck!* His hand went to his side and came away with blood. "Grenades!" he ordered again. He managed to get to his feet, staggering, but able to remove another grenade from its pouch. He pulled the pin.

As they prepared to toss them, most of the approaching men fell to the ground in an instinctive survival tactic. The dust and flying debris caused by the three grenades gave Bishop and his team time to turn and disappear into the forest. He figured they'd almost reached their destination when he collapsed.

"HEY, I'M ABOUT TO LEAVE, do you want me to bring anything?" Angel's gaze was fixed on the picture of Bishop and his team, the same one Diana had sitting on her mantle. Once Diana had found out about her and Bishop she'd had a copy made for her. Angel promised herself that the next time Bishop made it home she was going to get a picture of them together.

"Nope. I just made the pitcher of margaritas and everything else is done, just waiting for you to get your butt here."

Angel could hear the smile in Diana's voice. "Okay, be there in a few." She grabbed her overnight bag and headed out.

Ten minutes later she was turning into Diana's driveway. Angel always looked forward to their time together. They spent the evening eating chicken tacos with fresh guacamole, Tostitos, and home-made salsa. Diana had dug out a stack of old childhood photo albums of her and Bishop, and Angel lost herself in the pages while listening to the lively stories Diana shared with her. It gave Angel the chance to learn about Bishop as a boy, and then as a teenager. While they sipped tasty margaritas and laughed, Barnie, Diana's cat, moved back and forth between them, vying for attention.

"Sounds like you and Bishop had a terrific childhood." Angel sipped on what she deemed would be her last margarita before bed. She was feeling very relaxed.

"We have terrific parents," Diana said. "You'll meet them soon. They're coming next week to spend a few days."

"I'd like to meet them," Angel said, yawning loudly. "Sorry."

Diana yawned, just as loudly. They both laughed. "I think those margaritas are getting to us, and it is getting late. Ready to turn in?"

Angel nodded, rising unsteadily to her feet. "I know the way." She reached for her bag and almost toppled over, managing to catch herself in time. "Goodnight," she laughed softly.

"See you in the morning.

Chapter 3

It was early morning, and Angel was halfway between sleep and being awake. She hadn't opened her eyes yet, undecided if she was going to let the relaxing warmth of the covers lull her back into a deeper sleep. She felt a slight movement at her side, wondering how Barnie had managed to get inside her bedroom when she was so sure she'd shut the door. She started to turn to her side, away from him, when something soft brushed her nose. She brushed it away, smiling in spite of herself.

"Go away, Barnie." Her early morning voice sounded raspy. She made the turn and clutched the pillow to her, moaning. "I'm going back to sleep."

Angel figured a couple seconds went by before she felt him brush up against her ear. She moved her head away to break the barely-there contact. Knowing Barnie, she expected another swipe of his paw at any moment. He wanted attention, and he never gave up. When a soft, gliding touch appeared against her cheek, Angel released a sigh of resignation and rolled onto her back again. She knew the pesky cat wouldn't let up until she acknowledged him.

"Barnie," she groaned, reaching out blindly to rub him. "Be a good boy and I'll rub you down later."

"What if I want a rub down now?"

Angel's eyes flew open, locking instantly onto the amusement in Bishop's gaze. With a cry of surprise and happiness she pulled him down to her. "Bishop!" His mouth took hers in a long, rough kiss filled with hunger and warmth, sinking down on top of her. Any concerns she had had about him at that moment disappeared in a heartbeat. Angel welcomed his possession, opening her mouth to his seeking tongue, moaning low as his hands moved over her. The emotion of seeing him again was overwhelming, causing tears to burn in her eyes. By the time their passionate reunion was over he'd reversed their positions and she wound up on top of him.

"I didn't expect to see you again so soon," she said when she was able to talk. Because she was looking down at him her tears fell upon his face. "You kept your promise." She kissed them away, wondering if he'd remember what he'd said to her before leaving.

He did. "I never make a promise I don't keep." He sucked her bottom lip into his mouth. "I was going to surprise you in North Carolina, but Diana said you skipped your trip to the mountains at the last minute."

Angel nodded. "I decided the yard needed some major work and wanted to get it done before school starts up again." She shivered at the feel of his cock turning hard beneath her. "Did Diana know you were coming home?"

He nodded. "I'm glad I called her first. I missed you, baby. Damn, I missed you." Bishop's tone was rough with emotion, and his hands kept her hair from falling down around her face by holding it back by her ears. He closed the distance between them and kissed her again.

She melted against his cool, smooth mouth, tangling her tongue with his, loving the warmth and flavor of his mouth, and the texture. Bishop released Angel's hair and ran his hands down her back, over her bottom and the backs of her thighs before settling his hands beneath the curve of her butt. She was wearing a pair of bikini panties and it didn't take him long to slide his palms beneath the silk. He branded her where he touched her, dragging a moan of pleasure out of her.

No one affected Angel the way that Bishop did. She willingly gave him whatever he demanded of her, meeting him kiss for kiss, touch for touch. The month separating their last time together caught up to her, and she squirmed against his hard body, noticing for the first time that he was partially undressed and wearing a pair of boxer briefs and a white tank. His cock was hard as a rock and pounding against his shorts. She rubbed her hand over it, gaining another groan from Bishop as he bowed sharply into her hand.

As passion exploded between them lust ruled their desperate actions. Bishop's hands made quick work at removing what little Angel had on, before leaning back and whipping off his shirt. When his hands went to his boxers Angels hands were there, stopping him. He looked at her questioningly, breathing hard.

"Let me," she said huskily, getting to her knees. Completely naked, she was aware of his gaze burning over her while she lowered his boxers to expose his hard and throbbing cock. *Just like I remembered!* Bishop was well endowed. His dick was thick and long, and Angel's pussy constricted with remembrance of what it felt like stretching and sinking inside her body. Her breathing hastened as she reached for him, running her hand over the top where thick pearly pre-cum had gathered.

"Jesus!" Bishop rasped, shuddering wildly.

Angel smiled, leaning closer. "I missed you so much, Bishop," she admitted in a soft tone. "I kept myself busy during the day so I wouldn't think of you, but during the night . . ." she kissed her way up his neck to his ear, her hand caressing his dick the whole time. "At night you're all I dreamed about. I can't tell you how many times I woke with my nipples tingling, wishing your mouth was sucking them." Angel took the lobe of his ear into her mouth and tugged on it. "And my pussy wet and aching to be filled by your cock."

A growl rumbled from Bishop's chest and Angel found herself flat on her back in record speed, with him poised over her. She arched with hunger, encouraging him to complete the union. Their gazes locked and their breaths mingled as she anticipated his next move. When he finally moved, it was with slow precision designed to fuel and feed their desires at the same time. Mutual moans filled the room as his hot, rigid cock filled her to capacity.

Tears fell from the corners of Angel's eyes, falling to the pillow beneath her head.

"Baby—"

She shook her head. "I'm okay."

Bishop kissed the tip of her nose. "Then why the tears?"

"I'm just happy," Angel explained. "It feels so good, with you inside me again." She felt his cock pulsate, and she clenched her muscles around him in return.

Bishop groaned low and breathed against her lips. "Sweet Jesus, you're going to make me come just by doing that."

Angel smiled. "Doing what?" She clenched around his shaft again, holding it. He shuddered and closed his eyes. "That?" she asked mischievously.

It was clear that he'd caught the amusement in her tone as he opened his eyes again. "I'm going to punish you for that," he threatened in a hoarse voice.

"Do your worst," she challenged, unafraid.

With an animalistic sound Bishop slammed his mouth down on hers, pulling his cock out of her body. Her moan vibrated against his mouth. He slammed his hips forward, playtime obviously over, as he began to fuck her in earnest. Angel arched into every deep thrust of his cock, whimpering and moaning her satisfaction. She raked her nails down his back, clenching her hands into his firm buttocks.

"Feels so good," she said against his lips. Bishop was a good lover. He knew how to please Angel. It was more than just fucking, and had been since the very beginning. He made love to her, unselfish in his quest to see to her pleasures before reaching his own. Now was no different. His hand moved between them to her pussy, where he began to manipulate her clit until Angel was gasping and digging her nail into him.

"So warm and wet for me." His finger circled the swollen nub before pinching it.

"Oh!"

"That's it, baby," he encouraged as she twisted and cried out softly. "For a whole month I've dreamt of your sweet cum coating my fingers." He leaned down to take a nipple into his mouth.

"Bishop!" She felt the beginnings of her climax spiraling through every nerve ending in her body.

"I want to taste you, baby." He pulled his cock out and moved down her body. Then, lifting her hips, he pulled her forward onto his face. His tongue slid into her slick channel, tasting her excitement, withdrawing to lather her swollen labia. "So fucking sweet," he murmured, in between licks.

"Oh, God!" His words were just as powerful and effective as what he was doing to her body. Angel bowed into his intimate caress, the breath catching in her throat. Her world was spinning out of control at a rate that she couldn't keep up with. Her hips moved of their own accord, welcoming the invasion of his tongue and fingers, while her hands clenched into the sheet beneath them.

When Bishop's fingers discovered her G-spot Angel knew it was all over. She felt his fingers curl upward against the small, almond shape and torture her without mercy. All the while his tongue lavished attention on her clit and the sensitive, surrounding area. As the rush of an orgasm raced through her veins, she was helpless to do anything but let it go and enjoy the ride. "I'm coming, Bishop!" she cried, convulsing wildly. "Oh, God! Oh, God! "

He continued his administrations a few more minutes before kissing Angel's pussy lips and then taking her by the hips and flipping her over. She didn't need to be told to move into position, crawling to her knees weakly and thrusting her butt in the air. Almost immediately Bishop penetrated her drenched pussy, burying his cock to the hilt.

Angel whimpered her pleasure, trembling violently. "I love when you fuck me from behind," she said when Bishop started to move slowly. "The feeling is more intense."

He moaned and continued to thrust.

"I love the feel of your balls slapping against me," she added, pushing back every time he thrust forward. "And when your cum fills me."

"Fuck, Angel," Bishop swore, picking up speed and slamming into her forcefully.

She moaned, feeling another orgasm building. His hands reached around and covered her breasts, squeezing them and pinching her nipples. Overwhelmed by the different sensations gripping her, pain and pleasure combined, Angel closed her eyes and focused on Bishop and what he needed. She wanted him to come, but it was impossible to ignore the fire rushing through her blood, or the incredible ripples darting from her nipples down to her clit.

"Aaaagggghh!" His cry was guttural as he plunged into her one last time. He fisted his hands into Angel's long hair, pulling her head back so he could kiss her at the most crucial moment. As their lips moved feverishly against each other Angel felt his powerful climax inside her body. She instinctively clenched around his cock, getting a weak groan in response.

Bishop's breath was hot in her ear. "This is what kept me going the last month," he rasped, collapsing against her. He kissed the back of her shoulder.

"Sex?"

"Sex with *you*," he clarified. He slipped out and moved to the side of her, capturing her gaze. "You're the only woman I've ever taken with me on a mission."

Angel lifted on her elbows, smiling at his confession and knowing the significance of that. He'd told her once that she wasn't the kind of woman he liked to get involved with, preferring the kind who were only in it for the fun, sex with no strings attached. He didn't want any goodbyes, didn't want thoughts of leaving someone behind should he not return. Commitment to another person could mean mistakes, and death.

Yet something had clicked with them right from the beginning when they'd shared a bed out of necessity, and woken to a strong, mutual need. Their brief involvement had ended up being so much more than a casual fling. Though Bishop had tried to remain aloof, in the end he'd been forced to admit that there was more than just sex between them.

"So," Angel took a deep breath. "What now?" she finally asked.

Chapter 4

A knock at the door startled them both and kept Bishop from replying to her question. "Are you two ever going to come down?" Diana joked from the other side of the door.

Bishop chuckled. "If you know what's good for you, little sister, you'll go away."

Diana released a loud huff. "Well, there's coffee in the kitchen when you're ready."

Bishop reached for Angel and pulled her on top of him. He gently pushed the hair back from her face and kissed her. He'd meant it to be brief, but as soon as their mouths meshed and she opened her sweet lips to his tongue, he wanted to consume her. Crushing her against him, he savored the feeling of her naked body, her fresh warm scent, and her long silky hair surrounding them.

A groan escaped him when she began to caress his torso. She could easily get him in the mood again. He welcomed the exploration of her small hands, but sucked in his breath when they glided over the sensitive area of his recent injury. One surgery to remove two bullets and two weeks in the hospital for recovery had gone by agonizingly slow. They'd released him early, and he knew that his temporary medical leave could end at any time.

Angel must have caught his reaction because she stopped moving and lifted her head to look him in the eyes. Before Bishop could explain, she shifted her weight slightly and looked him over. There was a small furrow between her eyes as her gaze landed on the slightly puckered, pinkish flesh at his side.

"These are fresh." She glanced up, looking at Bishop with concern in her pretty eyes. He remained quiet. After a moment she leaned down and kissed the area. "You should have said something, I could have hurt you."

Something in her tone alerted Bishop to the fact that Angel was more than just concerned. There was no denying the disappointment and hurt in her eyes.

He knew why. "Baby, there's no way you can ever hurt me. And before you ask, I didn't tell you because it goes with the occupation. I've been wounded before and I'll probably get a few more scars before I've decided I've had enough." Angel remained silent, but the emotion swimming in her eyes said it all. *Damn it all to hell!* Her reaction was exactly the reason he'd remained unattached from commitment all these years.

Bishop knew he had to say it. "If we're going to make this work, baby, you have to understand that. I didn't even tell Diana, and had I not been released from the hospital early you would never have known, either. Most of the time I stay on base." Fisting his hand in her hair, he forced her down to his lips. Bishop kissed her long and hard, until he felt Angel's resistance melt away and she was sinking into him. He crushed her against him passionately before gently pulling her head back. "I had to see you, baby. I don't intend to waste any more time on base when I can be here in your arms." Even when he knew it was only for a day or two.

The small smile covering her face gave him hope that she was slowly coming to terms with how their relationship was going to work. Well, at least when it came to his obligations and decisions as a Navy SEAL. Bishop had been doing a lot of thinking about that, too. He wasn't quite ready for a change, but he knew it was coming.

"I'm happy that you're here, Bishop, but I'm sorry about your injury."

Bishop gave a toothy smile, not missing a beat. "How happy?"

Angel pushed at him playfully. "You look like a wolf about to make a meal of a helpless little lamb."

"Well, I am hungry," he growled.

"We can start with coffee—"

Bishop raised up enough to reach her neck so that he could nibble on her. "I think I'll start with you," he said between gentle bites. His hands traveled down to Angel's bottom, taking the flesh in his hands and pulling her closer to his erection.

"You've already had me." Her breathlessness revealed the state she was in.

An amused grumble vibrated through him. "*That* was just an appetizer." He ran his open mouth over her delicate shoulders.

Angel laughed huskily. "I hope I satisfy your craving." Her hands twisted in Bishop's hair, which was longer than he usually wore it. He found that he liked the feeling of her nails scraping against his scalp.

"You're like an addiction. You feed my need, and every time we make love I want you again even more." *When have I ever called "fucking" making love?* It surprised him that he meant it. What they were doing was more than lust-induced, or simply satisfying an itch.

As he kissed and nibbled his way over her satiny skin, his cock hardened enough to part the seam of her pussy lips and slip against her labia. They both released sounds of pleasure and strained further into each other. When Bishop felt her tight little nipples digging into him he knew that he had to taste them. As if reading his mind, Angel lifted the top half of her body and slid upwards until he could lock his lips around a plump breast. Taking as much flesh into his mouth as he could, Bishop slowly pulled back until nothing but the tip of her breast was in his mouth. Gently, he rolled and bit down on her nipple until she was moaning and squirming against him.

He didn't know how much longer he could take the feel of her loins grinding against his cock. Where he'd slipped between her pussy lips she was drenched and hot. Bishop moved onto her other breast, and when he was done loving it he pushed Angel back until they could make eye contact. Fire burned in her eyes, leaving her cheeks flushed and her lips parted as she panted. She sat up, giving him a good view of her frontal nudity. She was beautiful, all soft and curvy. He reached up and cupped her breasts.

"Ride me, baby." He thrust his hips up to encourage her.

Angel scooted back and took his cock into her hands. The feeling was exquisite. She ran her hand up and down his shaft, paying special attention to the sensitive head. The pre-cum pooling in the slit became lubricant, and when she leaned forward to kiss the tip of his cock Bishop lost it. His impatient growl must have alerted her that he was at his limit because she glanced up with a teasing grin and raised her body.

Bishop's gaze was glued to her delicious cunt as she slowly lowered down his cock. He couldn't help thrusting upwards to intensify the feeling. He closed his eyes when Angel clenched her muscles around him, releasing a groan that sounded like a mix of pain and pleasure. Her light laughter bounced around the room as she began to ride him with lazy restraint.

He let her have control for the moment, lying back and enjoying every little whimper that passed between her lips, every little change in her expression that told Bishop what she was feeling was honest and real. Reaching up, he caressed her breasts, tweaking the hard crowns of her nipples. His reward came when Angel reached behind her for his balls. She rolled them gently with her soft hands, stroking the embers that burned through his blood into an inferno.

"Oh, God, baby." He didn't even try to control the shudder that racked his body. "You're so snug and wet. I'm not going to be able to hold out for long."

She laughed huskily, obviously enjoying the power she held over him. As their eyes met and clung with smoldering heat, Angel began to move faster, little whimpering noises sounding in her throat. When she curved her body sharply, his gaze shifted to where their bodies were joined, becoming mesmerized with the sight of his cock penetrating her sweet depths. One hand moved down her body. Forming a V-shape with two fingers, he slipped it between her pussy lips and trapped her distended clit.

"I want you to come with me," he rasped, determined to hold back his orgasm.

"Oh!" Angel caught her breath when he began to move his fingers up and down, applying the pressure that would get her there. She continued moving up and down his cock. After a few seconds of his fingers pinching and rubbing the nubbin, her breathing accelerated and her movements became wild. "Bishop!" she cried out, her glazed-over eyes widening. "Come now!"

She didn't need to tell him twice. God in heaven, it felt great to release the burning ache in his balls. Forcing his dick in as far as he could, he came hard. "Aaagggghh!" Her body clenched tightly around him, drawing every drop of cum from his cock as they convulsed together in mutual release. For several minutes they were lost in the moment, gasping for air, twitching spastically, until eventually their bodies calmed and they returned to reality.

Chapter 5

"It's about time you two lovebirds made it down."

Feeling her cheeks grow warm, Angel exchanged an amused look with Bishop. He shrugged and turned back to Diana.

"We had to get reacquainted." His tone wasn't the least bit apologetic.

A brow rose. "It's only been a month." She moved to the coffee pot on the counter and poured them each a cup. "Thirty short days."

Bishop chuckled gruffly. "Thirty three days, and what's your point?"

She spun around with disbelief and humor. "My, God, you actually kept track of the days?" She finished pouring and turned back to them with a cup in each hand. "This has got to be a record short mission, and how did you get a second leave so fast?" She placed a cup in front of where they were sitting.

Angel wondered how Bishop was going to answer that. She made a show of putting cream and sugar in her coffee, ignoring Diana's eyes. They were close enough that she would know that something had happened, and Angel didn't want to be in the middle if Bishop came with a different story that was something else from what really happened.

"You're not happy to see me, sis?"

"You know I am."

"Then just be glad all is good and I'm here." He took a sip of his coffee.

Angel glanced up while taking a sip. Bishop gave her a wink. Diana missed nothing.

"You two are hiding something."

"Don't look at me," Angel grinned. Barney jumped up onto the island, meowing for attention. She gave him a lingering pat. "I'm not going to question what's turning out to be the best summer of my life."

"Mine, too, baby."

"So, how long do we have you for?" Diana asked, sitting down next to Bishop.

"I head back tomorrow morning. What have you got around here to eat?"

"Yogurt?" Angel asked, giving Bishop an amused look. She remembered his response when she'd offered him one for breakfast their first morning together a month ago.

"No self-respecting SEAL would be caught dead eating that girly stuff."

Her heart swelled. His exact words then. "Have you ever tried one?"

She went to the fridge, knowing Diana always kept it stocked with yogurt because she loved it, too. She reached inside for the first one her eyes lit upon, a fruity pineapple. A sharp whistle had her straightening when she realized her short robe had ridden up the backs of her thighs. She turned around to a wolfy look on Bishop's face, while Diana rolled her eyes. Angel got a spoon and walked toward him with determination.

"You're not going to get me to try it," he said with a smile in his eyes.

"Oh, oh!" Diana laughed. "A challenge!"

Angel stopped in front of Bishop and batted her eye lashes. He crossed his arms and raised a brow. "You can bat those long lashes all damned day."

Angel said nothing. She set the yogurt down and opened it. Scooped some onto a spoon and held the spoon up to him, batting her lashes again. Diana laughed, but Bishop remained unmoved. Angel took a bite, closed her eyes and groaned as if in the throes of an orgasm. When she opened them again it was to see the flash of fire in his. His expression grew taut with his obvious determination to stay unaffected. She held the spoon up again, closer to his mouth.

He shook his head. "Not going to happen, baby."

Angel stared at him for a moment, before reaching up and opening the top of her robe just enough to show some cleavage. Bishop's gaze was drawn there, and a muscle tightened in his jaw. She offered him the spoon again, with a smile of victory on her face. That was all he needed to see to take a deep breath and shake his head again.

"Good try, but I'm not going to give in to temptation."

He was tempted? That gave Angel an idea. She glanced at Diana. "You might want to turn around for this."

"Not on your life," Diana said. "I want to see who caves first."

"Don't say I didn't warn you," Angel replied. She met Bishop's eyes. Did he look nervous? Her smile widened, she'd get him to try it by playing dirty. "Oops!" The yogurt slipped off the spoon landing in her cleavage. His eyes darkened and the raw expression on his face spoke volumes.

Diana just groaned, turned around, and walked out of the room. "I'll be outside watering the flowers."

"You don't play fair, honey." He reached for her but Angel danced away from him.

"Are you ready to try some yogurt?" she said in a teasing voice. She opened her robe further, exposing her breasts except for the nipples. A chunk of pineapple slipped further down.

"What is that?" Bishop asked, watching it slide down between her breasts.

"Why don't you taste it and decide for yourself?" She smashed her breasts together, spreading the creamy mixture.

A low groan sounded through the kitchen and Bishop reached for her again, this time snagging the sash around her waist. Angel gasped when he jerked her against him. Then she moaned loudly when he lowered his head and began to lap up the yogurt. The warmth of his tongue as it scraped against her flesh left her tingling and excited.

"Mmm," he said, licking one breast clean and moving on to the other. "Not bad, baby. I think I could eat more of it, as long as you're wearing it."

The only thing keeping Angel on her feet was the fact that his hands were clutching the lapels of her robe. He lifted her up until she was on her toes, and continued licking.

"I think you've got it all," she breathed softly, highly affected by what he was doing. The way he had her up against his body made her aware of his hard-on.

"I just want to make sure. Mmm, pineapple." He looked up as he chewed, and then surprised her by pulling her close and kissing her. He tasted of warm sunshine and pineapple and it was over way too fast.

As they continued to look into each other's eyes she began to get the feeling that Bishop wanted to say something but was holding back. She knew that he had to leave first thing in the morning, and didn't want to think about it. His words about accepting things that way came back to her. She would wait for Bishop and take him under any circumstances.

Before either had a chance to say anything Diana returned, holding her phone out to Bishop. He took it wordlessly.

"Yeah?"

Angel met Diana's eyes for an explanation. She shrugged. "It's someone named Wizard. His team has my number for emergencies. Bishop must have left his phone upstairs."

Angel nodded, glancing back to Bishop. He remained unresponsive, quietly listening to whatever was being said to him. His expression turned grim and he pulled his eyes from Angel. A sinking feeling in the pit of her belly warned her that their brief time together might be coming to an end earlier than he'd planned. Why else would Wizard be calling him? She took a deep breath and braced herself for disappointment. He snapped out a few words, disconnected and handed the phone back to his sister.

"Wizard and the guys said to tell you hi." Angel nodded. "I've got to get back."

Angel forced herself to smile. They'd barely had one full day together, but she wasn't going to complain. The look on Diana's face revealed her own disappointment. Once Bishop walked out the door they would turn to one another for comfort. For the first time this summer Angel would be glad when school started again and her days would be filled with teaching kindergarten. At least Diana had Alex.

Bishop released a long breath. "You okay, baby?"

Angel nodded. "Would have been nice to have tonight with you but I'll be okay. Do you need any help packing?" she asked without thinking.

"Baby," he chuckled, "I didn't even unpack. Let me run up and get my bag. I'll be right back."

He was no sooner gone than Angel and Diana stepped into each other's arms. "I miss him already," Angel said against Diana's shoulder. She was not going to cry! At least until Bishop left.

"Me too, honey." After their embrace they sat back down. "I have a feeling he'll be coming home a lot more often now, when before he used to just hang out with his team wherever."

Angel hoped so. When Bishop returned he was carrying a duffle bag and was fully dressed. The expression on his face said that he wasn't any happier than she was about having to leave so soon. Their gazes met and clung as he set the bag down and continued to where she was sitting.

"I miss you already, baby." He took Angel into his arms and crushed her against him. "I'll be back as soon as I can." His comment was followed up with a long, thorough kiss that filled her body with the instant heat of desire. "You'll wait for me?"

"You have to ask?" Angel smiled, struggling to keep her composure.

Bishop turned to his sister and they exchanged brief hugs.

"Be careful," Diana said when they pulled apart. Her eyes were swimming with emotion.

"You know I will," Bishop responded. He picked up his bag and Diana and Angel followed him to the door.

"If I get the chance I'll call you before the team leaves."

Angel nodded. *God, I love him!* She wanted to say the words but held back, understanding that now wasn't the time. They stood at the doorway and watched him walk to his jeep. Angel was glad he didn't look back. She was barely holding on. He backed up in the driveway, giving them a last wave before driving away. Hot tears rolled down Angel's face as she stood there until he was out of sight.

"I'm going to marry that man some day, Diana," she said in a shaky voice, turning toward her friend.

"Huh," was Diana's response as she closed the door and turned to walk away. "Almost the exact same thing Bishop said when he called me the other day to ask me where you were."

Angel watched Diana disappear into the kitchen with blurry vision, a smile slowly widening on her face. *He said he was going to marry me some day?* Pure happiness enveloped her senses, and Angel made a promise to herself that the next time Bishop made it home she was going to tell him how she felt.

If he didn't already know.

THE END

THANK YOU FOR READING my book, I hope you enjoyed it. Leaving a review where you purchased it would be greatly appreciated. Continue reading for more information about me and my work including excerpts to some of my latest releases.

ACE - coming out late 2018

A road side bombing left Ace disfigured and dead inside. He faces the world with silent bitterness and a damaged ego. Then a quiet beauty comes into his life, cracking the shell around his wounded heart and healing his soul.

Ace is a member of the Sentinels. Both are standalone MC romances.

Phantom Riders MC Trilogy

Phantom Riders MC - Book 1

Betrayal leaves Hawk, president of an outlaw motorcycle club distrustful and hating woman. Once he's satisfied his animal urges he casts them aside without a second thought. But then Audra shows up, threatening his club and way of life and Hawk has to decide to turn the sexy pint-sized package of trouble loose, or claim her for his own.

No Mercy - Book 2

Rock's the VP of Phantom Riders MC. Dangerous. Unpredictable. Ruthless. A killer who'll stop at nothing to keep what's his. Allie had given Rock her virginity, and then ran away when she got pregnant. Club trouble doesn't stop him from showing up at her door seven years later, demanding his son, and claiming her.

What He Wants - Book 3

Big John...club enforcer. He's big and scary and he sets his sights on Daisy the instant he locks eyes on the curvy beauty. Daisy...she's grown strong and independent since leaving an abusive marriage, but nothing prepares her for the hulking, sexy biker who wants to claim her!

Nomad Outlaws Trilogy Book 1

R uthless - Book 1

Blurb - Wildman forced Rebel to take Ginger's innocence in a sick and twisted initiation to prove his loyalty. He helps her escape, and she disappears soon after, helping herself to his money first. Four years later he tracks the innocent beauty down, but it isn't just his money that he's after. He wants Ginger for himself, and he'll go to any lengths to claim her.

Dangerous - Book 2

Jace is a nomad, an outlaw biker who likes to work alone. Fierce, dangerous, a killer when he needs to be. He calls no place home, and no woman owns his heart. Until *her*. Luna.

Furious - Book 3

Moody had it all once, and lost it in a heartbeat. Now he goes through life as a cold, heartless nomad. A man to avoid and be afraid of, uncaring that each day could be his last. He gives a fuck about nothing and no one, until an innocent woman appears out of nowhere, unafraid of his fury, challenging his demons, making him want to live again. Is he strong enough to let her into his heart?

Phantom Riders MC - Hawk
Excerpt

I quickly scooted out of the booth, realizing Hawk was right behind me. Before I could question him, he grabbed my arm and proceeded to jerk me in the direction leading to the back of the bar. I glanced around the bar wildly, but I didn't see Dane's men anywhere.

"They left, but they'll be back." We entered a dark hallway and halfway down he stopped us at a door. I expected him to knock, but he lifted his leg and kicked the door in, causing the occupants in the room to scream out in fear. "Out!" he snarled.

I barely had time to acknowledge the naked couple before they snatched up their strewn about clothes and rushed past us. As the man passed me I recognized him as one of Hawk's men. We made eye contact long enough for him to wink at me. Once they cleared the threshold, Hawk pulled me inside and slammed the door behind him.

"Take your clothes off."

"What?"

"Take your clothes off."

I know my jaw dropped at his demand. When I realized that he meant it I began to back up, slowly shaking my head. "You're crazy!" I whispered sharply.

"Take your fuckin' clothes off!" So far he hadn't moved from his spot, yet I'd backed up until my back was against the wall. "Those men knew how to find you, which means there's a bug on you somewhere."

I tried to decipher what he was saying, but my brain wouldn't wrap around the words that he thought I had a bug on me. He took a menacing step toward me, and that was all I needed to do what he wanted. Strangely, I wasn't afraid of Hawk, only of what having his hands on me would make me feel. I was attracted to him in a strange way that left me feeling confused. Maybe it was because I knew that he wasn't attracted to me.

I quickly removed my hoodie and handed it to him, kicking off my shoes at the same time. As Hawk began going over it, I unzipped and rolled down my jeans. I'd reached for the bottom of my t-shirt when a memory slammed into me.

"Just a minute." I waited for him to look at me. "There's no way there can be a bug in these clothes because they aren't mine. I took them from a dryer in the laundromat."

He hesitated for only a second. "I want everything."

Deciding not to argue with him, I removed my t-shirt and threw it at him. He caught it to his chest and I swear I saw the tiniest curve of his mouth showing amusement at my irritation. He examined my clothes thoroughly, finding nothing, as I'd expected. Then he turned those dark eyes on me, running his gaze up and down my body, missing nothing.

"*Everything,*" he demanded. "Or did you borrow your underwear, too?"

No, the underwear I had on were mine. An expensive, sexy, thong and bra set Dane had purchased for me from Victoria's Secret. The way Hawk's gaze moved over me turned me on when it shouldn't have. I was no stick figure, my short height gave me curves I'd spent half my adult life hiding, until I'd realized that some men liked meat on their women. The coffee eyes on me now revealed that Hawk was no exception.

I swung around and reached up to unhook my bra, hearing Hawk's hiss. Tossing the bra to him, I waited, unsure if I would be able to remove my thong. This was silly because my backside was completely naked to him in that moment. I pulled it down, catching another hiss from Hawk when I bent slightly to work it over my knees and down my legs. I tossed it over my shoulder in his direction. Completely nude, I reached for the top sheet on the bed before facing him again.

"Satisfied?" I nearly swallowed my tongue when I saw that he had my thong in his hands. There was no way a bug could be hidden in that tiny, see-through thing.

Hawk's expression was savage. Something strong and basic controlled him. He reminded me of a bronze statue, solid and powerfully intimidating. I was a prisoner, held captive by the intensity in his eyes. Slowly his hand moved upward to his face, pausing right beneath his nose. His nostrils flared and his eyes closed as he crushed the bunched thong and inhaled deeply.

Ohmygod, I'd never seen anything so compelling, so erotic. Lust slammed through me, flushing heat over my whole body. I held my breath and watched as his eyes opened slowly, lazily, revealing the truth. He was as turned-on as I was. No, scratch that—he was *ravenous*!

"Toss me your shoes."

What? Was I reading him all wrong, seeing something I only wanted to see? But then everything I'd learned during my short acquaintance with Hawk came back to the surface, reminding me that he ignored his emotions and his body's cravings. I didn't think that he was afraid of letting go, he didn't strike me as a weak man, but as someone who thrived on absolute total control. That made him very dangerous.

I grabbed my Valentino sneakers and tossed them to him. He caught them with one hand. He examined them thoroughly, frowning when he came to the pyramid studs decorating the side. One of them appeared to be loose and with little effort he was able to remove it. He held it up for me to see but I had no idea what he wanted me to acknowledge.

"It's decoration."

He shook his head. "It's GPS."

Ruthless
Nomad Outlaws Trilogy Book 1
Excerpt

I GRABBED GINGER BY the hand and pulled her out of the room, down the hall and to the bathroom. Her resistance was futile, her fear unimportant. I knew what I had to do, and if she were smart, she'd realize it, too. If she wanted to live. I opened the bathroom door and yanked her inside, thanking fuck that I found it empty. It was filthy, but better than nothing, and it had a shower that everyone used when they felt the need to be clean, which wasn't often.

Ginger spun around when I shut the door, the look of a trapped animal in her pretty blues. I ignored her growing terror, steeling myself for what I had to do. Even behind closed doors I had to make it real, had to be convincing that I was an unfeeling bastard. I saw her swallow, could see her tits rising and falling rapidly as the fear of the unknown overwhelmed her. She was expecting the worst, preparing herself to do whatever she had to do to survive.

"Take off your clothes." I kept my tone harsh, indifferent to her growing panic.

She shook her head vigorously and stepped back, slamming hard against the cracked porcelain sink. A nervous cry escaped her, and her eyes were wild as she took in her surroundings and realized that there was no escape. Her gaze touched on the door behind me before meeting my eyes.

"Please-"

"Take off your fucking clothes," I said in an uncaring, demanding tone. "You're filthy, and not in a way that gets my dick hard. Now undress." I removed my cut and the t-shirt beneath it. "In fact, I think I'll join you." Her eyes nearly popped out of her head at that. "If you're not undressed by the time I'm out of my clothes, you won't like the consequences." I kicked off my boots as my hands went to the front of my pants.

As I'd expected she would, Ginger's small hands began to unbutton her blouse. Slowly she began to expose enticing, creamy skin to my wandering eyes. I undid my pants. She lowered her gaze to the floor and turned around before reluctantly removing the garment. I let her have her moment of modesty before I looked into the mirror in front of her. Fuck. My dick took notice of her perfect tits and rosy nipples. Hard nipples. Surprising.

Dangerous
Nomad Outlaws Trilogy Book 2
Excerpt

"WHAT'S THE HURRY, DARLIN'?" This came from the biker that I'd been hoping to avoid. Samson had moved away, and the man's hands were resting on top of his thick thighs as he balanced his bulk on his bike.

He was wearing biker gloves, the half-finger kind. As I glanced over the patches on his vest, I noticed that he had one on that said "Nomad", while the other bikers' patches revealed that they were in the Wreckers MC. His muscular bulk, the bulging muscles that I'd already noticed in his arms, revealed that he was a powerful man. He was nowhere near as handsome as the blonde God, but there was something about him that made him appealing, too appealing for my peace of mind. His square jaw and strong, firm mouth was sensual. Even though his eyes reflected friendliness, I got the impression that this man was dangerous and someone to be careful around.

"I'm hungry," I finally said, as if that explained everything. I ignored the chuckles of two of his friends, mesmerized by the steel blue of his eyes as they dropped down my body in a lazy assessment that stole my breath.

"Me too," he returned, his gaze roaming back up my body. "And you're just my type."

Instant heat flushed through me. He was teasing me, and I didn't like the quirk on his mouth. The way he was looking at me made me feel naked in my jean cutoffs and clinging t-shirt. As I felt my nipples betray me by hardening beneath his stare, I took a breath and forced myself to walk away.

"Sounds like your problem," I said indifferently.

There was no way I was getting involved with an obvious bad ass when I'd just gotten rid of one.

Well, one who'd thought he was, anyway.

Don't miss out!

Visit the website below and you can sign up to receive emails whenever Tory Richards publishes a new book. There's no charge and no obligation.

https://books2read.com/r/B-A-WTJ-PHYU

BOOKS2READ

Connecting independent readers to independent writers.

Did you love *Serve and Submit Series*? Then you should read *Kiss Me!*[1] by Tory Richards!

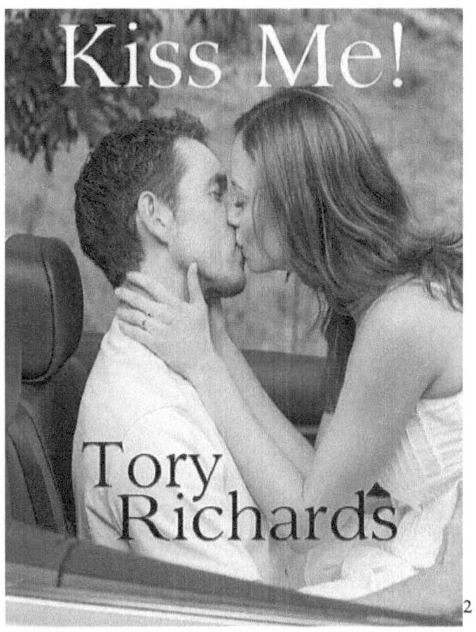

[2]

Two years after Emma's divorce she's looking forward to settling into a quiet life in her new condo at the lake. But thanks to her match making sister she's running into Stratton's sexy small town detective at every turn. The last thing Mike's looking for is a relationship to complicate his busy life, and tells Emma as much. So, if that's the case, why can't keep his hands off her?

Read more at www.toryrichards.com.

---

1. https://books2read.com/u/b62YwZ

2. https://books2read.com/u/b62YwZ

Also by Tory Richards

Desert Rebels MC
Cole
Demon
LD

Nomad Outlaws Trilogy
Ruthless
Dangerous
Furious

Phantom Riders MC Trilogy
Phantom Riders MC - Hawk
No Mercy
What He Wants

The Evans Brothers Trilogy
A Perfect Fit
Surrender to Desire

Burning Hunger

Standalone
Up in Flames
Bishop's Angel
The Mating Ritual
Out of Control
Wicked Desire
Someone to Love Me
Wild Marauders MC
Big, Black and Beautiful
Carnal Hunger
Dark Menace MC - Stone
His Possession
No Escape
The Evans Brothers Trilogy
The Sentinels
Hands-On
Kiss Me!
Obsession
Wild Surrender
All the Right Moves
Hers to Claim
Nothing But Trouble
One Night Only
Serve and Submit Series
The Cowboy Way
Ace
The Alpha Wolf's Mate
A Soldier's Promise
Taken by the Outlaw

Watch for more at www.toryrichards.com.

About the Author

Tory Richards is a fun-loving grandma who writes smut with a plot. Born in 1955 in the small town of Milo, Maine, she's lived most of her life in Florida where she went to school, married and raised a daughter.

Penning stories by hand at ten, and then on manual typewriter at the age of thirteen, Tory was a closet writer until the encouragement of her family prompted her into submitting to a publisher. She's been published since 2005, and has since retired from Disney to focus on family, friends, traveling, and writing.

Read more at www.toryrichards.com.